The Morning Watch is an account of a few hours in the life of a sensitive boy at a church school in the mountains of Tennessee. Two encounters in the early morning of Good Friday form the basis of the story. The first is spiritual: As Richard kneels in the darkness of the school chapel—his eyes on the guttering candles of the altar—he bursts suddenly and fervently on his God. The second, more secular, occurs on an unauthorized journey into the countryside where he directly confronts his physical environment and in awe and heartache learns something of its inexorable nature.

Through Richard's experiences, Agee shows us something of the inextricability of good and evil beauty, of the simple and the unfathomable. The story is clear on its surface but, beneath the surface, complex and ambiguous as a dream, and it is left to each reader to determine in his own way what is meant at this deeper level.

BOOKS BY JAMES AGEE

PERMIT ME VOYAGE

*LET US NOW PRAISE FAMOUS MEN
  (with Walker Evans)

*THE MORNING WATCH

A DEATH IN THE FAMILY

AGEE ON FILM
  (2 volumes)

*Published by Ballantine Books

THE
MORNING
WATCH

JAMES AGEE grew up in Knoxville, Tennessee, where he was born in 1909. He attended Phillips Exeter Academy and was graduated from Harvard in 1932. From 1932 to 1934 he was a staff writer on *Time*, where he wrote book and film reviews, cover articles and miscellaneous pieces. In 1943 he became motion-picture reviewer for *The Nation* and later wrote for films himself (*The African Queen, The Bride Comes to Yellow Sky, The Quiet One*). Among his works are *Let Us Now Praise Famous Men,* a study of the conditions under which Alabama tenant farmers managed to exist in the thirties, and the Pulitzer Prize novel, *A Death in the Family.* He died in 1955.

THE
MORNING
WATCH

James Agee

With an Introduction by
Alan Pryce-Jones

BALLANTINE BOOKS • NEW YORK

PREFACE

by
Alan Pryce-Jones

Men of letters are seldom attractive human be-
ings. I remember once being rebuked by Somer-
set Maugham for some small act of consideration.
It was a more or less humorous rebuke, but it
contained the stern warning that the better the
word "nice" applied to a writer the less good he
was likely to be in his art.

From time to time, however, there emerges a
writer whose "niceness" is balanced by a touch
of the intolerable. Everybody loves him; he
distills an irresistible attraction; he also maddens.
Shelley is an obvious case, and, in quite recent

times, Dylan Thomas another. Somewhere between the two stands James Agee.

To my sorrow, I never knew him; but I have known many of his friends. And one and all, men and women, they responded to him in the same way. Their defenses fell, they found themselves, if in differing manners and to different degrees, in love.

In love with a man who drank too much, and talked too much; who got into scrapes of the kind that occur when a sensitive conscience is unallied to a gift of self-discipline; who wove into a splendidly virile conduct of life so many unexpected strands of almost feminine hesitation?

Certainly. No less than Shelley, Agee deserved his Trelawneys. And some of the reasons which inspired such devotion can be discerned in the pages of *The Morning Watch*.

It could very easily have been a failure. Sensitive boys abound in fiction; they may influence people but they seldom make friends. Richard, in this short novel, is above all a sensitive boy, and he is steeped in an atmosphere as dense as it is, for

viii

most of us, unfamiliar: the atmosphere of a High Church school.

Agee's triumph is to set this truly awful school and Richard into a just perspective. He does so by taking both perfectly seriously. All easy ironies are rejected out of hand. Richard is, we must suppose, to some extent a projection of Agee himself at the age of twelve. Like Agee, he is fatherless; like Agee, he has found one trusted friend among the priests who run his school—it is tempting to see in Father Fish an echo of the real life Father Flye to whom Agee wrote a whole bookful of excellent letters. Again, like Agee, Richard is obsessed by a genuine if unfashionable problem: that of reconciling accredited behavior in this world with prospects for the next.

At this stage of life Richard accepts the Christian revelation. He accepts therefore—and the "therefore" is the key to the book—a need to qualify for sainthood. For the jogtrot Christian he has no time at all. The occasion for proving to himself that he possesses the necessary dedication is during the Morning Watch of the book's title: the Easter vigil in his school chapel. "In hidden vainglory he had vowed that he would stay awake straight through the night." These are the opening words of his story, and they contain the essence of what is to come.

Richard's problem is, I have said, taken seriously by Agee. But it has to be seen in the framework of school life. And here Agee does a very brilliant piece of, as it were, camera work. The focus upon Richard is not identical with that on the school. Richard is not only a small boy, he is also what the other small boys call, without much affection, "a crazy kid." Agee thus, and without overstressing their orneriness, adopts a different focus for Hobe, Jimmy, the athletic Willard and the rest, not to speak of the priests who rule their every thought—at least in principle. It is they who have to set the norm, Richard who has to be the exception. It is possible at times to think that Agee, writing twenty-five years later, looks back on his own youth with too strict a reproach, yet Richard never quite loses our sympathy.

The book is very carefully composed. For some tastes the prose may be almost too sonorous, the descant of mystical aspiration almost too piercing. But Agee saves the day every time by, on its own small scale, a Shakespearean counterpoint between the level at which Richard operates and that of the groundlings who bob in and out of his story. It is as though his one night's drama were peopled by a single hero and a chorus of fools.

Not that Agee fails to see the funny side of Richard. Adolescent piety can easily look funny to a grownup, and it has needed all the tact of a most tactful writer to preserve Richard's human dignity.

It is only at the end that we see him in full perspective: that we can sense in him something like an Agee-to-be. There would be little difficulty in building a symbolic superstructure on the last pages of the book. The boys have come out of church into the beginnings of dawn. Instead of doing as they have been told and going back to their dormitory they go off for an illegal swim in the Sand Cut. There two things happen. Richard finds a locust shell, ". . . transparent silver breathed with gold . . . the face of a human embryo." And later on, when the boys disturb a snake, it is Richard the "crazy kid," the sissy, who kills him, much against his own will. Furthermore, this is no ordinary snake, ". . . for it was clear that he had just struggled out of his old skin and was with his first return of strength venturing his new one." Richard is almost worshipful with admiration of such cold and elegant splendor, yet he kills him just the same. The snake's blood lies on his hand, and ". . . he began to feel that he had been brave in a way he had never been brave before and he wanted the hand to clear gradually and naturally, the way the smudge clears from the forehead on Ash Wednesday."

Yes, one might say, I see it all: the unfolding world is experienced only by playing truant from a superior duty. And then the locust shell, so beautiful, so dead, so nearly human in its desolation; and the snake with its recollections of Eden. And had there not been some hogs by the school door, as though to recall the warnings of Hieronymus Bosch? And is there not a notion of sacrifice, no, an even subtler notion of sacrifice-to-come, in the reference to Ash Wednesday?

I do not say that such deductions are illegitimate, but I suspect that Agee meant nothing so explicit. He is telling not only a story but a fable, and it is the fabulous side of Richard's story which counts for him. The boys make much of their expectation of punishment when they break the rule and slip off for a swim, but we never know what reception they were given when they returned. That is because, in a fable, such terrestrial matters are unimportant. What matters is the exemplary aspect of Richard's conduct, his renewed efforts, his slippings back, his mental confusions. Retribution, in some form or other, will come anyway, as it did to the locust, simply as a concomitant of being alive.

The little book was published in 1951, having first appeared in *Botteghe Oscure*, the notable review directed by Marguerite Caetani in Rome. But as early as 1945, Agee was writing to Father

Flye that he had ". . . started a short novel about adolescence in the 1920's—a fairly good start. But in ten days I haven't come back to it. And by now it looks too flimsy. With so little time from work and so very little time left for anything faintly recognizable as civilization, it seems rather too obligatory to work only on the best things possible. But those are even harder to hold to— for anyone of my weak will. I started a book about the atomic bomb. . . ."

From these lines alone one can see that plenty of Richard survived in his creator a generation later. The snake had revenged himself. Some day a study will be made of those writers who were born into Agee's generation. On either side of the Atlantic the same story will be retold: of the fate which lay upon those born shortly before World War I. It was not a wholly hostile fate. In fact, few generations have put greater talent into the world. But there is a vast gap between those born into the security of the late nineteenth century—say, Rupert Brooke—and those who arrived twenty years later. To grow up around

1905 and around 1925 was to belong to utterly different civilizations, and there is no question but that Agee was deeply marked by the *Zeitgeist*.

He was a young man of the Depression, a young man of the Spanish Civil War; a contemporary, within two years, of W. H. Auden and the so-called Pylon Boys of the 1930's. Admittedly, a writer of that precise moment who also lived in the United States could in theory shrug off some, at least, of the tribulations of Europe. That he could not shrug off the tribulations of his own country is amply demonstrated by his *Let Us Now Praise Famous Men*, superbly illustrated, and, in its later reissue, introduced by Walker Evans.

The Morning Watch is a more mature, if slighter, work. *Let Us Now Praise Famous Men* is almost too rich in texture, too willful in design. By the time he came to write his next book he was more watchful, more selective.

But he remains throughout a too-short life the child of his period. Where his contemporaries elsewhere slaked their reforming energies by taking up the cause of Socialist Germany, or anti-Fascist Italy, or Loyalist Spain, Agee was confined by choice and necessity to a single country —his own—in a time of transition. He transplanted himself from his native Knoxville to New York; he had small experience of Europe at first hand; he became involved in the pressures of earning a living the hard way—as a journalist and script writer. There was the drink, there were the wives, the women. And all the time much of Richard survived; not the childish Richard taking a dogmatic religion at its face value, but the shadowy saint who stood behind a disobedient child.

Not to have known Agee is to miss a keen sense of his essential goodness. But among those who did know him that sense appears to be universal. If self-destructive, he was certainly not destructive of others by overt intention. He could not suppress, it seems, a radiance which regularly cut through the cigarette smoke surrounding him. Was it that, unlike the older Hart Crane or the exactly contemporary Malcolm

Lowry, he never lost the gift of a saving laugh?

If, in the sum of things, he is destined to be part of American mythology—as, in different fashion, is Hemingway or Gertrude Stein— it is the force of his character which must compensate the paucity of what he wrote out of a sense of vocation, as distinct from much first-rate journalism. The importance of *The Morning Watch* is not only that it is an excellent short novel, but that it also offers, with great simplicity, a series of keys to the Agee myth.

THE
MORNING
WATCH

THE
MORNING WATCH

I

*My soul fleeth unto the Lord
before the morning watch: I say,
before the morning watch.*

—PSALM CXXX

IN HIDDEN VAINGLORY he had vowed
that he would stay awake straight through
the night, for he had wondered, and not without
scorn, how they, grown men, could give way to
sleep on this night of all the nights in their life,
leaving Him without one friend in His worst

hour; but some while before midnight, still unaware that he was so much as drowsy, he had
fallen asleep; and now this listening sleep was
broken and instantly Richard lay sharp awake,
aware of his failure and of the night.

Too late: already it was time: now it was the
deepest hour of the deepest night. Already while
he slept, with wrathful torches and with swords
and staves they had broken among the branches
of the Garden; Judas, gliding, had stretched
against that clear Face his serpent's smile; Peter
in loyal rage had struck off the dazed servant's
ear and He in quiet had healed him: and without
struggle had yielded Himself into their hands.
Could ye not watch with me one hour? No Lord,
his humbled soul replied: not even one: and three
times, silently, gazing straight upward into the
darkness, he struck his breast while tears of contrition, of humility and of a hunger to be worthy,
solaced his eyes, and awakened his heart. O yes
it was an hour more deep by far than the Agony
and Bloody Sweat: no longer alone, unsure; resolved, and taken. That was already fully begun

which could come only to one ending. By now He stood peaceful before Pilate, the one calm and silence amid all that tumult of malice and scorn and guile and hatred and beating of unhabitual light through all the sleepless night of spring; while in the dark porchway, even at this moment, the servant girl persistently enquired of Peter and he in fury and in terror denied his Lord: now the bitter terrible weeping and now, saluting this mortal morning, the cock's triumphal and reproaching cry. A deep, deep hour. Soon now the sentence and the torment, the scourging, the mocking robe, the wreathed, wretched Crown: King of the Jews.

O God, he silently prayed, in solemn and festal exaltation: make me to know Thy suffering this day. O make me to know Thy dear Son's suffering this day.

Within Thy Wounds hide me.

Suffer me not to be separated from Thee.

From the Malicious Enemy defend me.

By a habit of their own, meanwhile, his hands searched and tested along the undersheet, and now they told him that this time he had wet the bed so little that by morning nobody would know. He let out a long thankful breath and looked down along his bed.

All he could see at first throughout the long room was a kind of gelatin glimmer at the alcoved windows, and the aisled ends of the iron cots at right angles to his own: but when the foot which had awakened him lifted from the yielding board and it creaked again he saw in his mind's eye, large and close, the coarse-ribbed shambling stocking, flecked with lint, and knew that Father Whitman must be very tired; for to judge by the hissing sound, his feet scarcely left the floor. He wondered whether Father Whitman was sleeping at all, tonight.

Father Whitman touched a foot and whispered: "Quarter of four."

"Okay Fathuh," Hobe Gillum said in his clear hard voice.

"Quiet," Father Whitman said sharply.

"Okay Fathuh," Hobe whispered.

24

Now that the priest came nearer as silently as he could between the ends of the cots, Richard could see the tall ghostly moving of his white habit.

Father Whitman stopped at Jimmy Toole's cot, touched his foot, and whispered: "Quarter of four." Jimmy mumbled something in a light sad rapid voice and stuck his head under his pillow.

Father Whitman stepped between the cots and touched his shoulder. "Quarter of four," he whispered more loudly.

"Cut it out," Jimmy whined in his sleep.

Richard heard Hobe's knees hit the floor.

Father Whitman shook Jimmy's shoulder. "Quarter of—"

"*Quit* it you *God damn*—" Jimmy snarled, wrenching aside the pillow; then, with servile Irish charm: "Aw sure Father, I din know it was *you* Father."

At the far end of the dormitory there was a wild stifled snicker.

"Time to get up," Father Whitman whispered.

The snickering became happier and happier. Father Whitman spoke more loudly into the darkness: "Now cut that out fast or you'll be sorry you ever started it."

The snickering persisted as if uncontrollably, but now it was blunted in a pillow. Father Whitman ignored it. "Better get straight out of bed," he told Jimmy. "You'll go back to sleep."

Hobe was buttoning his shirt.

Without a word Jimmy rolled out of bed onto his knees and buried his head in his arms.

Now that Father Whitman came toward him, Richard shut his eyes. When he knew he was about to be touched he opened his eyes and whispered, "All right Father." He saw the stopped hand and, much nearer and larger than he had expected, the beaten, enduring horse face; he became aware of his deceitfulness and was ashamed of it.

"All right," Father Whitman said. Bet he says quarter of four, Richard thought. "Quarter of four," Father Whitman said.

"Yes Father."

"Put your shoes on downstairs," he whispered, and turned away. "Put your shoes on downstairs," he told Hobe, "and don't let Jimmy go to sleep again."

"Okay Fathuh," Hobe said, gallusing himself into his overalls.

"And don't you dawdle when you're done," Father Whitman told him. "You kids see to it you come right back here to bed."

"Yes suh Fathuh."

"Don't think I won't be watching for you."

"No suh Fathuh."

Richard knelt by his cot and sank his face in his hands. O God, he prayed, I thank Thee that I did not wet the bed this night—enough to get caught, he added carefully, remembering Thou God seest me; for Jesus' sake Amen.

He said swiftly to himself the prayer Father Weiler had taught them as enough when, for any good reason, you did not have time enough for more: I praise my God this day I give myself to

27

God this day I ask God to help me this day Amen.

Gripping his hair and pressing the heels of his hands tightly against his closed eyes he tried as hard as he could to realize what was happening as he had in the moment of waking. But now he could realize only what a special night this was, what grave and holy hours these were. There seemed to be a strange stillness and power in the air as there always was on very special occasions and never at ordinary times; it made him feel dry, light of weight, very watchful, expectant and still, and it almost made his scalp tingle. It was something like the feeling of his birthday, and of Christmas, and of Easter, and it was still more like the feeling he now seldom and faintly recalled, during the morning just after he learned of his father's death, and during the day he was buried. But it was not really like any of these, or anything else, except itself. These were the hours of Our Lord's deepest Passion. For almost forty days now this feeling had grown and deepened, not without interruption, for he had not managed perfectly to keep either his public or his secret Lenten Rules; yet he had been sufficiently earnest and faithful, and sufficiently grieved in his failures, that the growth had been deeper and more cumulative and more rewarding than he had ever known before; and now he was coming into the heart of it, the holiest and most solemn of its shrines, with heart and soul prepared and eager. Already it was no longer Maundy Thursday, the birthday of the Eucharist; that sorrowfully jubilant magnificence was turned under the world; already the world was brought a few hours forward into the most gravely majestic of all days, Good Friday; already the wheel was so turned that high upon darkened heaven white Easter dazzled, suspended, the crown of the year, like the already trembling start of an avalanche. Easter was very soon now, so soon, with his throat brimming with its hymns and his soul ardent for release and celebration, that it was difficult to be patient; yet his faith and absorption were such that at the same time he came into this day as sorrowing and careful as if Christ had never been crucified before, and could never rise from the dead. Yet now that he desired to retrieve his waking awareness he could not, but only knelt, sad, trying to taste the peculiar quality of the night and to distinguish it from other auras of momentousness, until, realizing how he had misled himself, he gripped his hair and pressed his eyeballs the more tightly, repeating in his heart: Jesus our Lord is crucified. Jesus our Lord is crucified. He saw the Head.

Thrown with fury, a shoe struck the wall next Jimmy's bed: the noise broke upon Richard with sickening fright. Then Hobe's voice:

"All right some mothuf - - - - - sonofabitch is agoana git the livin s - - t beat outn him if I find out who throwed that!"

"Shet yer God damn mouf," said a coldly intense, deeper voice at the far end of the dormitory.

"Yeah fer Chrise sakes *shut up*," said another voice, as several neutral voices said "Shut up."

In the rigid silence Richard and Jimmy dressed quickly while Hobe waited. Carrying their shoes they stole barefoot on tiptoe from the room and along the hall and past the iron cot which had been set up by the stairhead for this one night for Father Whitman. They could just make out how he lay there in the dark in his long white habit, giving off a current of silent and ominous power because they could not be sure as they passed whether he was asleep or aware of them; the clacking of his tin clock filled the pine stairwell with its flagrant loudness. They tried hard not to creak the stairs. The pit of Richard's stomach still felt as it did when, without being too mad or too desperate to care, he knew it was impossible not to fight. By trying hard he was able to restore whole to his mind the thorn-crowned image of his Lord, but now it was not as he had seen it in prayer beside his cot but was very little different from a pious painting he knew: the eyes rolled up in a way that seemed affected, and in his cold sickness the image meant little to him. It was not until they came onto the back porch that the open night put them once more at their ease.

"Sonofabitch mothuf - - - - - bastud," Hobe said. "At shoe bettah be gone by mawnin or *some* bastudly cocks - - - - -'s agoana be sorry."

"Aw shut up Hobie," Jimmy said. "This ain't no time to talk like that."

"Hell do *I* keer," Hobe said. "*I* hain't been to Confession yet."

But he started on down the steps without saying anything more.

"What happened?" Richard asked.

"Jis trine wake up Jimmy," Hobe said. "God All Mighty Christ, can't even wake nobody up in this friggin School—"

Richard followed them down the steps. He was glad he had learned hardly even to think of saying anything. If Jimmy told Hobie to shut up and quit cussing Hobie would take it off of him, they were buddies; but by now he knew enough to keep *his* mouth shut. He felt uneasy, though, because he was glad he had not sworn. That was like being thankful you were not as other men and that was one of the worst sins of all; the Pharisee.

He had forgotten all about the shoes he carried
and now that unexpectedly, for the first time this
year, he felt the ground against the bare soles of
his feet it was as if, fumbling among clothes in a
dark closet, he had put his hand on living flesh.
Even though the ground in this schoolyard was
skimmed with dusty gravel, its aliveness soared
through him like a sob and lifted his eyes in
wonder upon the night. There was no moon and
what few stars were out, they were made faint by
a kind of smiling universal milky silence, not fog,
or even the lightest kind of mist, but as if the
whole air and sky were one mild supernal breath.
Downhill in the Chapel a line of small windows
meekly smoldered, dark orange; he followed his
companions and saw that they too were carrying their shoes. When they came to the lawn beyond their building they left the gravel; the
ground, with its scarce new grass, felt like a fish.
There was a thick oak near the center of the lawn
and Hobe and Jimmy, as they passed, stung it

several times expertly with gravel. It had not occurred to Richard to pick up gravel and now he
was glad, for he was sure he would have missed
as often as hit.

THE
MORNING WATCH

II

THE NIGHT SMELLED like new milk; the
air which exhaled upon them when they
opened the side door of the Chapel was as numb
and remote as the air of a cave. Without knowing
it they hesitated, subdued by the stagnant darkness and its smell of waxed pine and spent incense.
Across the unlighted nave the open door of the
Lady Chapel brimmed with shaken light; but
just at their left, through the door to the vestry,
came a friendlier and more mundane light, a de-

licious smell, and the tired grinding of the voice they most admired in the world. When he became aware of their hesitation beside this partly closed door, George Fitzgerald spoke to them with a formality as unaccustomed and gentle as if a dead body lay in the room behind him and they came in, silent and shy. By the loud hurrying little clock it was still only four minutes to four. They squatted on their bare heels against the wall and looked on, their six eyes emphatic in the sleepless light.

The inward wall of this long corridor was hung solid with cassocks and they were of all lengths from a size almost big enough for the giant sad boy they all called Undertaker, to the all but baby size of Dillon Prince. At first Richard wondered where all the cottas were; in the laundry for Easter, he realized. The room was so weakly lighted by candlestubs that at the far end it was hardly possible to distinguish the red cassocks from the black. Just within the surer light, his jaw and his shoulders sloping more heavily even than usual with fatigue and with his low posture, Wil-

lard Rivenburg sat on a folding-chair which gave
out dangerous splintering noises whenever he
stirred. It was he who was talking, aimlessly,
quietly, almost in his sleep; and Richard could see
that George and Lee Allen answered him only so
often as courtesy required, never turning their
attention from their work. Not only were they
Prefects; it was also believed by some of the older
people that they alone among the boys now at the
School might have a Vocation. They were in
their last year now and it was generally under-
stood that they were both praying hard for this
to be made clear to them before they graduated.
It was their privilege, tonight, to trim and change
the candles and to remove and replace the withering flowers, and now white-girdled, incongruous
in red cassocks, they stood wearily beside a soup
plate, replying gravely in short words while, their
eyes bright with the lateness of the hour and fixed
in the profound attentiveness of great scientists,
they revolved candlestubs between thumb and
forefinger, just above a flame, and watched the
meltings add themselves to the already consider-

able cone of wax and tallow which they had developed on the plate. The shining melt spilled
roundly, rambling and congealing; wherever it
ridged, they smoothed it delicately with their
fingertips. From the apex of this rounded cone
sprang three long fiery wicks.

Because they were to be up all night these two
had been forgiven the fast and had supplied themselves against possible hunger. But neither had
yet eaten or drunk, nor did either privately intend
to unless, as seemed unlikely, he became too faint
or too sleepy to attend properly to his share of
the work. Their coffee frothed so noisily over its
can of Sterno rather because this enhanced their
feeling of privilege and maturity; Willard was
drinking some while he talked although, Richard
reflected, it was long after midnight, when the
fast began. He had also practically finished off a
box of Fig Newtons.

The coffee was so strong that it empurpled the
wall of the cup, and its smell was almost as envi-
ably masculine as that of white lightning. The
three younger boys kept respectfully quiet and

looked on, eagerly and sleepily. They watched now the lapped purple rings in the slanted cup, now the shining of the living wax and its satin look where it had slowed and had been smoothed, now the strong loose smoky flame and the hypnotized faces which leaned above it, and now the reckless primitive profile and the slash-lined blue-black cheek of the great athlete Willard Rivenburg, whom they had never seen in quite such quiet intimacy. Nobody knew for sure just how old Willard was, but he looked as many men can only at thirty or so, and then only if they have been through a war, or years of the hardest kind of work. Richard tried to imagine why he was here tonight. He was fairly sure it was not for any kind of religious reason: Willard had been confirmed, and made his Confession and his Communion, but it was obviously just as a matter of course; when he took his turn serving Mass or swinging the Censer or carrying the Crucifix he was never exactly irreverent yet he always looked as if secretly he might be chewing tobacco; it looked as odd and out of place, somehow, as

39

watching a horse dressed up in cassock and cotta
and doing these things. He never even crossed
himself at a hard time in a game, the way some of
the others did. No, he wouldn't be here because
he felt pious. It might be because everybody and
everything on the place was thinking about just
these things that were happening, and moving
around them; a kind of shadow and stillness came
over everything during Holy Week and it might
be that Willard felt this and was made uneasy by
it. But mainly it must be just that he was much
too grownup to be able to stand all the silly rules,
and tame hours, and good behavior, that were expected of living in a school; he must be even
gladder than the little boys were to grab at any
chance to break out of that routine, especially
anything that would give him an excuse for staying up so long after hours. And yet, Richard reflected, Willard needed and took an awful lot of
sleep, dropping off in dull classrooms or where-
ever he had to sit still, except for eating, as easily
as a colored man or a dog. But maybe all that
sleep was why he was able to be awake now,

though as a matter of fact he wasn't really more than half awake, not nearly as wide awake as Richard felt. But then probably he had been up all night, and probably it wasn't for the first time in his life either.

In some way which it did not occur to him to think about or try to understand, Richard felt a warm rich comforting kind of pride in him and sense of glory as he watched him, as much, in a far quieter and even happier way, as when he watched his almost magical ability in sports; and he began to feel a sense of honor and privilege in having this surprising chance to be so near him and to watch him so closely, to really see him. For normally, when Willard was not playing or practising or sleeping or eating, he was kidding with somebody, in a loudly reckless, crazy way which was a pleasure to see because everything Willard did was a pleasure to see, but was impossible to see through; but now he wasn't kidding at all, only talking quietly and steadily like a grown man, among others whom he treated as grown men. He was finishing up about his grandfather who had come over from Switzerland to settle way back on the Mountain and who had never bothered to learn much English, and he was saying the few words and phrases of German he himself knew, and Richard was deeply impressed in realizing that Willard, who always seemed to him to know about as little as anyone could, except as an athlete and captain of genius and a powerful and experienced man, actually knew words in a foreign language. He himself was accustomed to feel a good deal of complacency because with Father Fish's help he had learned several hundreds words of French, but now he felt ashamed of himself, and resolved to learn German, which seemed to him a much more virile language.

He was watching with shy and particular interest the hump between Willard's heavy shoulders, which he had often wondered about but never yet had the chance to examine so privately. It was almost as if Willard were slightly hunchbacked, the low way he always carried his head and sloped his shoulders and the way this hump bulged out just below the base of his neck; yet if he were deformed, he could not have such ability and strength. It must be a very greatly developed muscle, Richard realized, yet it was a funny place to have a muscle; he felt there now on his own body and there wasn't even the beginning of a muscle there; just bone. Could it be bone? But that would be a deformity; and on Willard, more than any other thing, it was what made him unique among others, and marked his all but superhuman powers. Whenever he had done anything physically creditable Richard carried his head low, let his mouth hang open, and tried to hump his back, scarcely knowing of it any more; and so, though it was not generally realized, did many other boys in this school.

"Hey you," Lee said, and startled, they looked: one minute past four. Richard felt a spasm of shame: could ye not watch with me one hour? Besides, they were keeping somebody over his time. "*Jesus!*" Hobe Gillum said, and they stood up quickly. Both of the boys in cassocks ducked in shocked acknowledgement of the Name and

43

Willard's dark face brightened with his satanic parody of falsetto laughter. Lee Allen said with unusually kind gravity: "I sure would hate to have to report anyone for cussn right in Chapel, and on Good Friday too." Hobe's eyes turned Indian, with pride towards Willard, in defiance towards Lee. "Aw forget about it, Lee," George Fitzgerald said, "he just wasn't thinking." "I don't want to report you or nobody else," Lee said. "You just watch your mouth, Hobie." "He didn't mean anything," Richard said; and even before everyone looked at him and said nothing, he was miserable. "Better put your shoes on, you kids," George said, and with relief Richard sank his hot face over his shoelaces. They felt contempt for him, he was sure, and he felt contempt for himself. Willard thought better of Hobe for cussing than of him for standing up for him, and so did he. Lee jumped on Hobie because Willard's cackling about it bothered him and he couldn't jump on Willard. If it hadn't been Good Friday and Richard had spoken up like that he knew that somebody would have said coldly, "Well look who's talking." Keep your mouth shut, he kept whispering within himself intensely. Just keep your fool mouth shut. And as they left the room he tried to exorcise the feelings of injustice, self-pity and pain by crossing himself quickly and surreptitiously. Fine time to go worrying about your*self*, he sneered at himself.

The nave replied to their timid noises with the threatening resonance of a drumhead. Not even the sanctuary lamps were lighted, but the night at the windows made just discernible the effigies and the paintings and the crucifix, no longer purple veiled but choked in black, and the naked ravagement of the High Altar. The tabernacle gawped like a dead jaw. By this ruthless flaying and deracination only the skeleton of the Church remained; it seemed at once the more sacred in dishonor, and as brutally secular as a boxcar. To cross its axis without the habitual genuflection felt as uneasy as to swim across a sudden unimaginable depth, and as Richard turned and bowed before the central devastation he realized: nothing

there. Nothing at all; and with the breath of the
Outer Darkness upon his soul, remembered the
words: And the Veil of the Temple was rent in
twain.

But here in peace and victory before the adoration of all creatures past and breathing and
uncreated, shrined and enthroned, starred round
with unabating light and with the stars of all the
fields of spring as well, exiled there yet abides
throughout this night the soul and substance of
the everliving God Who shall, within these few
hours now, be restored to His High Altar and
there devoured, leaving His whole Church dese-
crate and unconsoled until the hour of His glori-
ous Resurrection from the Dead. Tied in its white
veil, stifled, a huge masked Head, a thinly clouded
Sun, the monstrance stood from the top of the
tabernacle and broke at its center a dense tissue
of flowers and light: candles it seemed by thousands, spear-high and merely tall, and short, and
guttering, each an abiding upright fiery piercing
and, crisp and wearying, withering, dying, the
frugal harvest of the dawn of the year: from faint

orchards the last apple blossoms, still tenderly
raveling their slow-borne blizzard; branches of
mild-starred dogwood and of the hairy wild azalea, pink and white, from the mulled gray woods,
and little fistfuls of those breathless violets which
break the floor of winter, even the rare mayapple,
the twinleaf, whose bloom stays just a day; and,
of the first shivering domestic flowers, cold jon-
quils, crowds of them, greenish with chill or
butter yellow or flaming gold, and clear narcissus,
reaching, bowing, staring, fainting in vases and
jars of metal and glass and clay and in drinking
glasses and mason jars and in small and large tin
cans, all these each in their kind and sufferance
bore witness before God while they might. Few
of these early flowers have strong fragrance, or
any, yet the heat and the brightness and the fragrance brought forth by the burning wax and
tallow and by the heat in the closed room, all one
wall of dizzying dazzle, were such that it was at
first almost as difficult to breathe the freighted
air as to breathe water, and this air was enriched
the more by the devotions of those who knelt

subsumed within the trembling light; and at the
instant of stepping into this hot and fragrant gold,
going upon one knee and gazing upon the blind
rondure of the monstrance and the thousand-
pointed blossoming of fire and flower, his heart
was lifted up and turned vague and shy as the
words broke within him, upon each other, God:
Death; so that the two were one. Death: Dead,
the word prevailed; and before him, still beyond
all other stillness, he saw as freshly as six years
before his father's prostrate head and, through
the efforts to hide it, the mortal blue dent in the
impatient chin. He remembered within this instant how for the first time he had been con-
vinced, and how eternally convincing it had been,
when he saw how through that first full minute
of looking his father had neither stirred nor spok-
en, and how the powerful right hand had lain half
open against the exact center of his body; the
cloth of his coat was not moved by any breathing
and it was as if the hand were only a magically
expert imitation of a hand, a hand of wax and,
now looking again at the head, lips and a face of

48

wax, a dent of wax, a head of wax immense upon this whole rich waxen air. Dead, the word came again, and shutting his eyes he prayed swiftly for his father the prayer of all his childhood, God bless daddy and keep him close to Thee and may light perpetual shine upon him, Amen; and casually, obliviously, as a trout into shadow, the image and memory vanished. It is Our Lord's death today, he said to himself, but at this moment he could see neither face, that of his father, or that of his Lord; only the words returned, God: Death.

No praying-benches were available at first, and they knelt where they entered, the waxed floor brutal against their bones. In the Name of the Father and of the Son and of the Holy Ghost, Richard whispered rapidly to himself, moving his lips and closing his eyes again. He crossed himself with care. There was a sound of arising and departure and through his eyelashes he saw Knox Peyton complete his genuflection and step ungainly between him and Jimmy, trying to subdue the reproach and annoyance in his face. They stayed where they knelt, all on their good manners before the one empty bench, and Richard heard the whispered "go on" several times before he realized that it was directed at him. Two worshipers glanced unhappily behind them, shut their eyes, and tucked their chins down, trying hard to pray. "I be damned if I will," Richard thought, and caught himself; he shut his eyes tightly and in despairing shame tucked his own chin down. "Go *on*," he heard. He decided that he ought to make a penance of it. Trying to look and to feel neither humble nor proud he crossed himself, got up, genuflected, tiptoed to the empty bench, genuflected, knelt, and crossed himself. Mr. Bradford closed his eyes, frowned, and deeply bowed his head. Home stretch, Richard said to himself, and quickly begged forgiveness for an irreverance which had not been premeditated but spontaneous. But wasn't it even worse to be so unaware of where you were that such a thought could occur spontaneously? Mr. Bradford completed his devotions and tiptoed towards the door, his eyes downcast. His effort to stay within himself was too successful; Richard heard him bump against one of the two boys, and his whispered accusing apology, and their feckless and ill-subdued reply. Deaconess Spenser, at the desk opposite his own, compressed her lips, crossed herself, got up, genuflected, and stepped behind him; he could hear the harsh whispered reprimand whistling through her false teeth. He looked carefully at his clasped hands, but he heard movements as the door was cleared and along the side of his eye Jimmy advanced and swiftly established himself at the newly empty bench and the Deaconess, her wattles a violent red and her mouth pulled in tight, returned to her own bench, genuflected, knelt, crossed herself, and sank her forehead into her hands. Behind him somebody else stood up and he heard the knee touch the floor and, knowing he ought not to, glanced back; it was Hog Eye Kelsey, one of the littler boys from his own dormitory; already Hobe was standing to replace him. Not Hog Eye, he told himself; he can't help it: Jeff.

Pay attention, he told himself. Mind your own business.

He looked at the veiled monstrance; the brightest threads of the veil sparkled like mica, gold-white on silver-white, and in one place a rigid shaft of metal radiance almost pierced the fabric. One azalea bloom strayed against it as if it were straining to be near it. Tiny threads sprang out of the flare of the blossom, the way small straight lines are drawn in a funnypaper to show music coming out of a horn. An appleblossom fell. Looking at the tired sleepless flames of the candles, Richard felt as if he could almost hear them burning.

Soul of Christ sanctify me, he prayed silently; Body of Christ save me; but he was just saying it mechanically, and too fast. Slowly now, thinking carefully of each word, he began again.

Soul of Christ sanctify me: make me holy: absolve me from all spot of sin:

Body of Christ save me: save me: Thy Body which has already begun to suffer and die:

He braced his mind.

Blood of Christ inebriate me:

Carefully as he tried, he could not avoid it. Inebriate meant just plain drunken, or meant a drunken person, especially habitual drunkard, and as it was used here, it meant to make drunk, to intoxicate. And inebriety meant drunkenness and the habit of drunkenness. He had been fond of the word for a long time before he knew, or realized that he did not know, its meaning—which must of course be simply what the Blood of Christ might most naturally be expected to do: but what would that be, that sounded as nice as inebriate? During the past winter it had occurred to him to look it up in a dictionary. Since then the correct and disconcerting meanings had been indelible, and that part of the prayer had become thin ice. He could only get past it without irreverent or skeptical thoughts by saying it so fast or so shallowly that it was impossible to bear its meaning in mind, and that was no way to pray. He had asked Father Fish about it and Father Fish had shown him that it was possible to be amused by the word without feeling irreverent. He had said that some of these ancient prayers were rather extravagant in their way of putting things, and that there was no need to take them with absolute literalness. Although he had no way of being sure, Richard had a feeling that Father Fish had been as amused at him, as at the word; once again he wondered why, and stopped himself from wondering why because this was no time to. Don't take it literally, he told himself firmly; but the literal words remained and were even more firm: make drunk. Intoxicate. Good ole whiskey, he suddenly heard in his mind, and he remembered how, drinking sodapop in Knoxville, boys slightly more worldly than he would twist the bottle deep into the mouth and cock it up vertically to drink, and taking it down, breathless, would pat their stomachs or rub them in circles and gasp, "Ahhh, good ole whiskey!" But this wasn't even on whiskey. On blood. Jesus' blood, too. His uncle had once sneered, "There is a pudding filled with blood," scornfully exploding the first syllable of "pudding," and Richard had been both shocked and amused, and he was shocked to find that he remembered it with amusement now. Forgive us our trespasses, he whispered, shutting his eyes tight. It was only a hymn, and so it was not as bad to make fun of as some things were. But the blood was "drawn from Emmanuel's veins," so that did make it pretty awful. And his uncle had said it with a kind of hatred which included much more than the hymn: all of religion, and everybody who was religious, even his own sister, Richard's mother, and his Aunt Patty, and him, Richard, and his own sister. Forgive us our trespasses as we forgive those who trespass against us, he prayed, and pushed the matter out of his mind. He does like us all the same, he reflected, same as grandpa does. They just don't like the Church.

Passion of Ch——

Water from the side of Christ wash me; and he felt that his thoughts badly needed washing:

Passion of Christ strengthen me:

Within Thy Wounds hide me, he thought swiftly and with great uneasiness, hugging the

ground and the leaf coverage as if beneath the
skimming of a bird of prey: but try as he could,
the image plunged and took him. An older boy,
the only one Richard knew who also liked to
read, had with great sophistication and delight
explained to him what was meant, in Shake-
speare's *Venus and Adonis*, by the words *he
saw more wounds than one*, and this had instantly
become identical in his mind with a rawly inti-
mate glimpse he had had, three or four years before, of Minnielee Henley when they were
climbing a tree; and now with these words *within
Thy Wounds hide me* the image fought in his
mind with the image of those small but deadly
wounds in the body of Jesus, in which surely nobody could hide, not even the one the spear made
in His side. But not there either, he insisted to
himself; not even if He wasn't a man. Yet there
in his mind's eye, made all the worse by all the
most insipid and effeminate, simpering faces of
Jesus that he had ever seen in pictures, was this
hideous image of a huge torn bleeding gulf at the
supine crotch, into which an ant-swarm of the

pious, millions of them, pleading and rolling up their eyes, laden souls, by thousands meekly stealing, struggled to crowd themselves, and lose themselves, and drown, and dissolve.

It was the Devil, that was all. Just the Devil Himself, tempting him.

O good Jesu hear me, he prayed with deep self-loathing, almost aloud: and realized with gratitude that for once he had been able to say these words, which for months now had seemed to him fulsome and insincere, with complete desire and sincerity. You just have to mean it, he thought, for it to mean anything.

Suffer me not to be separated from Thee (a mortal sin is a sin that cuts us off from God):

From the Malicious Enemy defend me:

Of these closing lines he never felt doubt and now he repeated, with reverent emphasis and relish:

From the Malicious Enemy defend me:

In the hour of my death call me and bid me come to Thee:

That with Thy

No there was something really wrong about

He prayed, with fear and determination: That with Thy Saints I may praise Thee, forever and ever, Amen.

All the same it was wrong for people to ask to be saints, as flat as all that. Or even just to be *with* the saints, if that was what it meant. To just barely manage through God's infinite mercy to escape burning eternally in the everlasting fires of Hell ought to be just about as much as any good Catholic could pray for; and now Richard remembered still another prayer at which, when he was serving at Mass, he had for quite a while now been accustomed to keep silence or at most to make approximate sounds of the words, with his fingers crossed: where, in the General Confession, reviewing his iniquities, the penitent cries. "The remembrance of them is grievous unto us, the burden of them is intolerable." As a rule he was able to say "the remembrance of them is grievous unto us" with adequate sincerity; but it was seldom that he could feel, at the particular moment he felt required to feel, that "the burden of them

is intolerable." It wasn't anywhere near intolerable, no matter how much it ought to be. At first
he had been able to say it in the realization that it
was intolerable to his soul, whether or not he in
his mind and feelings was capable of feeling it just
then, and that prayers are said by and for the soul,
not the mind or the feelings; but in this he came to
feel that he was mistaken: for it was, he noticed,
only when he believed and felt deeply with his
mind or his emotions that he was able to be aware
that his soul, as such, existed. But that isn't true,
he now thought with alarm. No matter what I
think or feel, the soul is always there and always
alive unless it has been killed by impenitence for
mortal sin. The hardening of the heart towards
God. I'm only trying to suit myself, he told himself; not my soul, and not God.

But how can you say things when you only
ought to mean them and don't really mean them
at all?

Have mercy upon us O God have mercy upon
us, he found himself praying. These were the
words of the Confession which followed "the

burden of them is intolerable," and always, as now, he was able to mean them when he spoke them.

But not "that with Thy Saints I may praise Thee."

Now it occurred to Richard that perhaps this prayer had been written by a saint or by someone near sainthood, who was able to mean every extreme thing that was said; and he knew that anyone who could fully mean those things, and who could mean them every time they were said, was to be humbly respected. But in that case it was a prayer which was good only for saints and near saints to say, not for ordinary people, no matter how good they hoped to be. Nobody's got any business even hoping he can be a saint, he told himself.

God no! he exclaimed to himself, for now suddenly it became vivid and shameful in his memory that he himself had for a while cherished, more secretly even than his lust, exactly this inordinate ambition. Good golly! he whispered within his soul, feeling the back of his neck and

then his cheeks go hot; and with a cold and marveling, compassionate contempt for the child he
had so recently been, he lost himself in reflective
remembrance, unaware that it was for the first
time in his life.

It was hardly more than a year ago, when he was
only eleven, that the image and meaning of Jesus
and the power and meaning of the Sacraments
and of the teachings of the Church, all embodied
and set forth in formalities of language and of
motion whose sober beauties were unique, and in
music which at that time moved and satisfied him
as no other music could, had first and, it had
seemed, irreducibly, established upon all his heart
and mind their quality, their comfort, their no-
bility, their sad and soaring weight; and, entering
upon his desolation of loneliness, had made of
suffering a springing garden, an Eden in which to
walk, enjoying the cool of the evening. It had
become a secret kind of good to be punished,
especially if the punishment was exorbitant or un-
just; better to be ignored by others, than accepted; better still to be humiliated, than ignored.

He remembered how on mornings when he had waked up and found his bed dry, he had felt as much regret as relief. He had begun to take care to read in conspicuous places, where he would be most liable to interruption and contempt. He had pretended not to know lessons he had in fact prepared, in order that even such teachers as thought well of him, or thought "at least he's smart," or "he studies, anyway," might think ill of him. He had continued his solitary wanderings in the woods until it occurred to him that these excursions, for all their solitude and melancholy, were more pleasant than unpleasant; from then on he had put himself into the middle of crowds, especially on the drearier afternoons when even the hardiest boys stayed indoors and the restive, vindictive, bored, mob feelings were at their most sullen and light-triggered. The leaden melodies of the Lenten hymns had appealed to him as never before; lines in certain hymns seemed, during that time, to have been written especially for him. *Jesus, I my Cross have taken*, he would sing, already anticipating the lonely solace of tears con-

cealed in public: *all to leave and follow Thee;
destitute, despis'd, forsaken*, were words especially dear to him; *Thou from hence my All shalt be.*
As he sang that he felt: nobody else wants me;
and did his best to believe it, even of his mother.
He remembered now that this kind of singing
had satisfied him most at Stations of the Cross, on
cold rainy nights. *Perish ev'ry fond ambition*,
he would sing magnanimously; (no I *won't* become a naturalist; I'll never explore the sources
of the Amazon; I'll never even own a monkey, or
be junior tennis champion); *all I've thought or
hoped or known;* then tears and their subdual re-
warded him. *Yet how rich is my condition* (never
to live at home again, never to be loved or even
liked), *God and Heaven are still my own;* and he
saw crowned God and Heaven shining and felt, in
a humble kind of way, that he literally owned
them. Now remembering it he shook his head almost as if in disbelief, but he knew it had been so.
Everything. He had done just about everything
he could think of. He had gone seldom to Father
Fish's cottage, for friendliness was certain there,

and often cookies and cocoa too, and he had found that these luxuries meant most to him, in his desire to suffer for religious advantage, only when they were indulged so rarely that even while they were being enjoyed they enhanced the bleakness of the rest of living. He even schemed to intensify his always all but annihilating homesickness to the utmost possible, asking permission of the Master of the Day the more often, that it be the more curtly or impatiently or, at best, contemptuously refused; watching his mother's cottage, the one place he was almost never allowed to go, sometimes by the hour; sometimes in ambush under dripping trees, relishing the fact that only he knew of the miserableness of that watch; sometimes openly, hanging against the fence, relishing the fact that she knew, and others could see, and that even though she knew, she would try to ignore him and stay out of his sight, and that when at last she could ignore him no longer, she would hurt him by trying to be stern with him as she told him to go away, and would sharpen his unhappiness into agony by her idea of a sensible explanation why this senseless cruelty had to be law. "Because dear, mother thinks it's best for you not to be too near her, all the more because you miss her so much." "Because your father—isn't with us." "Because mother thinks you need to be among other boys Richard. In charge of men." And worst of all: "I know how hard it is now but I know that when you're older you'll understand why I did it, and thank me for it." *Thank her!* his heart sneered now, in bitter paroxysm. And for a moment so brief that the realization did not stay with him, he felt hatred and contempt for his mother, for her belief in submissiveness and for her telling him, on certain infuriating occasions, that it is only through submitting bravely and cheerfully to unhappiness that we can learn God's Will, and how most truly to be good. God's Will, he thought now. I bet it isn't just for people to be unhappy! Who wants to be *good! I* do, he answered himself. But not like that. I sure was crazy then, he thought, pleased that he was now able to recognize the fact. Just a crazy fool. The whole crazy thing had begun to fade away soon after Easter, with the good weather, and had vanished so completely during the free summer in Knoxville that he had forgotten the whole of it until just now: but all through that dreary winter and increasingly throughout that drizzling season of penitence, he realized now with incredulous and amused self-scorn, he had ever more miserly cherished and elaborated his wretchedness in every one of its sorry ramifications, as indispensable to the secret, the solution, he had through God's Grace discovered; and had managed easily to forgive himself those parts of his Lenten Rule which he meekly enjoyed in public, by inventing still other, harder rules which were private. His mother had tried uneasily to suggest to him that there might be a kind of vanity mixed up in his extreme piety —"not that you *mean* it, of course, dear"— against which he must be on his guard; but remembering the role of dismayed parents and scornful villagers in the early lives of many of the saints, he had answered her gently and patiently, with forbearance, that was the word, as befitted

communication between creatures of two worlds
so unbridgeably different. He had been tempted
on more than one occasion to say to her, "Wom-
an, what have I to do with thee? Mine hour is
not yet come"; but he had suspected that this
might be thought impudent or absurd or even
blasphemous. Nor had he ever said aloud, when
others jeered or tormented, "Father, forgive
them, for they know not what they do"; but had
often fortified himself with the silent words,
"And He held His peace."

It had only gradually been borne upon him that
he himself might aspire to actual sainthood; he
had quickly realized that if that was to be his goal
it was necessary, starting young, he might already
be too late, to perform in private for God's eyes
alone and in public that others might see, and be
edified, and remember, and revere him, a long and
consistent series of remarkable spiritual feats. Let
your light so shine before men that they may see
your good works and glorify your Father,
Which is in Heaven. But meditating what these
might be, he had realized that there in truth he

did run the danger of sinning through Pride, as those people do who look hungry when they fast; whereas his own ambitions were prompted (or so it seemed) by true religious feeling and by nothing else. These ambitions had crystallized during the late weeks of Lent, into a desire to do for Jesus as much as Jesus was doing for him and for all souls. He had experimented with extra fasting, but it was not possible to carry this far, since it was virtually impossible to be excused from meals without the sin of lying, and almost as difficult, he found, to sit at the table without eating, or eating little enough to give the fast any dignity or meaning. So he had chosen self-mortification instead. He had gone into the woods and eaten worms, but this had disgusted him, and he had been even worse disgusted when, on one occasion, he had come near tasting his own excrement. It had suddenly struck him as very doubtful indeed that Jesus would ever have done any such thing, and he had thrown the twig deep into the bushes and had carefully buried the filth. Efforts to scourge himself had been moderately painful but

not sufficiently effective to outweigh the sense of
bashfulness, even of ridiculousness, which he felt
over the clumsiness of the attempt, in relation to
the severity of the intention. So he had been re-
duced, mainly, to keeping very bitter vigil over
his thoughts and his language and over his sensu-
ous actions upon himself, and to finding out times
and places in which it would be possible to kneel,
for much longer than it was comfortable to kneel,
without danger of getting caught at it. (He had
been as frightened, once, by such interruption, as
if he had been surprised in a sexual act.) It was
during one of these protracted and uncomfortable sojourns on his knees that his mind, uneasily
strained between its own wanderings and efforts
at disciplined meditation, had become absorbed
in grateful and overwhelmed imagination of
Christ Crucified, and had without warning
brought to its surface the possibility of his own
crucifixion. He had been wondering with all of
a sincere heart how ever he might do enough for
the Son of God Who had done so much for him
when suddenly, supplanting Christ's image, he

saw his own body nailed to the Cross and, in the same image, himself looked down from the Cross and felt his weight upon the nails, and the splintered wood against the whole length of his scourged back; and stoically, with infinite love and forgiveness, gazed downward into the eyes of Richard, and of Roman soldiers, and of jeering Jews, and of many people whom Richard had known. It was a solemn and rewarding moment; but almost within the next breath he recognized that he had no such cause or right as Jesus to die upon the Cross: and turning his head, saw Christ's head higher beside his own and a third head, lower, cursing; and knew that he was, instead, the Penitent Thief.

But it was of course out of the question that in a deep country part of Middle Tennessee, in nineteen twenty-three, he could actually manage to have himself nailed to a Cross; and although (if he should have the courage) he could undoubtedly nail his own feet, and even one hand (if someone else would steady the nail), his right hand would still hang free, and it would look pretty foolish beside a real Crucifixion. With any proper humility he would be content merely to be tied up, as the thieves usually were, and to hang during the three hours of Good Friday that Jesus hung on the Cross. Even that would mean a good deal, if only in token; the widow's mite, only it seemed rather more than the widow had managed; and he realized that many others besides himself would be moved, and impressed, and very likely improved, by the good example. It would be impossible of course to get a Cross without removing the image of Jesus from it, that big life-size one out in the vestibule, and that would be irreverent even if it were allowed. Or someone might make one for him but he doubted it. He might make one for himself if he could sneak into Manual Training Shop and get enough private time, only everybody knew he wasn't any good with his hands and simple as a Cross must be to make, they would just laugh at any that he would be likely to make. One of the school's gridiron bedsteads would be convenient for tying to, and very likely even more uncomfortable to hang

71

against than a Cross, but he was forced to doubt, as with the nail-holding and the Cross, that he could manage the whole tying-up by himself, and as he thought of asking someone else to help him, he felt extraordinarily shy. As he singled over each of the few whom in any degree he trusted, or on whose affection he could at all depend, he became sure that there was not one who would co-operate in this, or even really understand about it. It would be necessary instead to anger and deceive people he disliked into doing it; but that, he felt, was both unlikely and sinful. If he got them mad they would do what they wanted to him, not what he wanted them to do, and he could not imagine how to suggest to them that the one thing he didn't want was to be stripped of his garments (except for a loincloth) and tied to a bedstead for three hours. And even if he should manage to, he would be tricking them into a sin, and that would be a sin of itself. It was easier just to imagine it as something already done, and as soon as he forgot about the problems of getting it done it was better, too.

There he hung, the iron bars and edged slats of the bed acutely painful against flesh and bone alike; but he made no complaint. Rather, his eyes were fixed steadfastly upon the expiring eyes of his crucified Lord, and his own suffering was as naught. There was a steady murmuring of scorn, pity, regard and amazement beneath him, and now and again a familiar face and voice was lifted, pleading with him or commanding him to come down. Father McPhetridge, the Prior, his wide red face reared up and told him that this was the most outrageous thing that had ever been done by a boy in this School and that he was to stop it immediately and come down and take his punishment like a man. He replied, gently and calmly, his voice all the more effective because of its quietness after all that indignant roaring, that "punishment" (he smiled at the word in his suffering) would have to come at its own good time; he would descend (with their help) promptly at three o'clock and not before; and would give himself up to his punishers without making a struggle. Scourge me, he said; paddle me with the one

with holes in it; put me on bounds all the rest of
the year; expel me even; there is nothing you can
do that won't be to the greater glory of God and
so I forgive you. The Prior, abashed, withdrew;
Richard saw his whispering among the other
monks and the teachers and his face was redder
than ever, and their whispering eyes were on him.
The football coach Braden Bennett, who had so
often sneered at his music lessons; his face was
changed, now: though with a scornful wonder,
men see her sore oppressed. He looked straight
back into those bullying eyes, with such quiet
fortitude and forgiveness that the scorn and the
wonder deepened, the wonder even more than
the scorn. His mother pled with him to come
down; she was even crying; and he was awfully
sorry for her; but he shook his head slowly and,
smiling gently, told her: "No, Mother, I deeply
repent for making you cry and feel so badly, but
mine hour is not yet come." She collapsed with
sobbing and the women of the place crowded
around her; they took her arms and helped her as
she walked away, all bent over. Some day you'll

understand, he told her within himself, and you'll thank me for it; and he knew the happiness that comes only of returning evil with good. Willard Rivenburg's deep dark jaw hung open and Richard could overhear his whisper, to Bennett, "Jesus that kid's got guts." George Fitzgerald, scarcely able to contain his tears, held up a sponge soaked in vinegar, which Richard forgivingly refused; and Hobe Gillum and Jimmy Toole and Parmo Gallatin and Keg Head Hodges and the others looked at him, glum but respectful; even if it was no more than politeness, he realized, he would never be last again, when they chose up sides. Through the half-open Chapel door he could still hear the voice of the Three Hour Sermon, Father Ogle's voice, and he realized that the service had no more than an hour, at the outside, to go; but the voice sounded half-hearted and sailed hollowly around the almost empty Church; nearly everyone in the community was gathered here in the vestibule, and there were some even from nearby towns, and suddenly a photographer climbed onto the sandstone font and aimed at him and flashed a bulb. STRANGE RITES AT MOUNTAIN SCHOOL, he read: and, as blood broke scalding upon his nape, sank his face into his hands and prayed, in despair, *O God forgive me! forgive me if You can stand to!* . . .

For, musing upon his past vanities with affectionate scorn or even as with a scornful wonder, the scorn, the living vanity, of one who has put away childish things, and dwelling upon them in remembrance, he had dwelt once more within them (within Thy Wounds hide me), ensnaring himself afresh. For these later imaginations were not wholly remembrance; some were newly his, and only now, even in the very hour of Christ's own passion, he had yet again seduced his soul. If others, if any other in the world, should know those absurd imaginations of his heart: by his dread and horror in the mere thought, he knew his contemptible silliness. But God of course knew, and Christ Himself, even now when the Son was suffering and the Father, grieving that He might not take the Cup from Him, was hovering in love and sorrow, yes, engulfed, enchanted in woe though They were, They knew very clearly though, it now occurred to him, his secret was safe with Them. In insupportable self-loathing he squeezed his eyes so tightly shut that they ached, and dug his chin as tightly against his throat as it would lock and in blind vertigo, scarcely knowing his action, struck himself heavily upon his breastbone, groaning within his soul, *the burden of them is intolerable.* With the second blow he realized, in gratitude and in a new flowering of vainglory, that he had been surprised into contrition so true and so deep that beside it every moment of contrition he had ever known before seemed trivial, even false, and for an instant he questioned the validity of every Absolution he had ever been granted. Yet almost before this question could take form, and even while his fist was preparing its third assault against his inordinate heart, this new doubt was supplanted by a recognition that his action was conspicuous and that it must seem to others as affected, as much put on for outward show, as

he himself, observing others, had come to feel
that various mannerisms in prayer must be. Bring-
ing his fist against his breast in circumspection he
opened his eyes, raised his head a little, and without turning his head, glanced narrowly around
him through his eyelashes.

Nobody seemed to have noticed anything out
of the ordinary although he could not, of course,
be sure of those who knelt behind him. He bowed
his head again, twisting it a little to the right,
lowered his right shoulder and drew it back a
little, and observed from nearly closed eyes. He
still could not see those who knelt directly behind him but so far as he could see, nobody
seemed to have noticed him; then he caught Hobe
Gillum's coppery eye, and blushed. He read-
justed his head and shoulder and watched Claude
Gray, who knelt a little ahead of him and to the
right. Claude's head was flung far back and was
so twisted in adoration that the point of his left
jaw, bright gold in the candlelight, was the most
conspicuous and almost the highest part of it.
What was more, it was clear that he was praying,

not to the Blessed Sacrament, but to the small, shrouded statue of the Blessed Virgin above the lavabo table; and noticing now for the first time that a little cup of violets stood on the plaster ledge at her feet, Richard was sure who had searched them out among the wet dead leaves to honor that place. He looked at Claude again, particularly at the tilted curly back of the head and at the abandoned angle of the brightened jaw, and thought, He may really mean it, he may not even know it but I bet he does, I bet he knows it makes a picture and I bet he got it from some picture of some saint or other. But if he did really mean it, and no longer knew he was doing it, then it was not fair to blame him. He was probably thinking about his mother. It seemed a long time ago he had lost his mother to keep on making so much fuss about it but maybe he took things harder than most people. Richard suddenly felt deeply ashamed of himself in case Claude really was grieving and praying for his dead mother, and he began to feel pity for her and for Claude as well, but then he remembered Claude's voice, which sounded more girlish than a girl's even though it had changed, reciting to him the Litany of the Blessed Virgin in impassioned sugary tones; O most clement O most holy O most sweet Virgin Mary; something of that sort and a lot more besides. He had felt uneasy about the whole thing and at the instant that Claude brought such juicy emphasis to the words *mosst sweett*, with such meticulousness about both t's and pronouncing *most* like *moused*, Richard had decided that he definitely disliked the whole prayer; and looking at Claude now, he disliked it even more thoroughly, and he decided that even if Claude was genuine now in his praying, he did not trust that kind of praying. He remembered his mother's gossiping about Claude once, his desire that the School should put lace borders on the cottas and his special attentions to the Blessed Virgin, and saying impatiently, "Well what I can't see is, why doesn't he just—go on over to Rome!"

But now remembering the scorn and impatience which had been in her voice, and still watching Claude, with the long hair of the back of his head like a shabby chrysanthemum, tilted above the weak neck, he felt that Claude was pitiful, and that it was careless and cruel to think of him contemptuously, and as shameful to be watching him in this way, so unaware that he was being watched, or that he might look in the least silly, so defenseless, as it would be to peer at him through a keyhole. How do *I* know, he thought, he's probably praying all right, and even if he isn't I've got no right to look at him like this and——

With this, something he could not quite remember, which seemed to be prodding at the edges of his thought, came abruptly clear. He remembered that he had started looking at Claude, and speculating with mistrust about the quality of his praying, because he himself had done something, without affectation, which might easily be misunderstood to be affected. He could not quite understand it but he was in some ignoble way trying to put off onto Claude something that was wrong with himself, or even worse, was assuming that Claude was doing wrongly what he knew

he himself had not done wrongly; and worse
even than that, he had so wandered and so lost
himself in speculating about the weakness of
another that he had degraded and lost his own
moment of contrition, and had forgotten the
very sin for which he was contrite, in committing
still another sin of much the same kind. But now,
although he could see the first sin, and the moment of contrition, and the second sin, quite
clearly, they formed something more like a picture than a feeling, and there were too many
things in the picture for him to look at any one of
them really closely. He felt shame and a sort of
astonishment. He wondered whether he would
ever learn, from committing one sin, how not to
commit another of the same sort even in the very
moment of repenting it; and he felt that it was
strange, and terrible, that repentance so deep and
real as he knew that his had been, could be so
fleeting. He felt deeply sorry and was filled with
self-dislike as he saw what he had done, but he
knew that the feeling was of a much shallower
kind than that in which, without foreseeing it, he

had struck his breast so hard. He thought of Jesus suffering on the Cross, but that deep and truest contrition was not restored; he looked again at Claude's unpromising head, and felt a mysterious sadness, which he could not quite understand, for whatever was imperfect and incompetent: Claude; poor little Dillon Prince, with his square-bobbed tow hair and his pink lashless eyes, forever crying or just over crying or just about to cry; a hen, with a wry neck which could never be straightened, standing as if shyly to herself in one corner of the chicken run, with one wing hunched; his own imperfect and incontinent mind and spirit; and again of Jesus upon the Cross, suffering and dying that all such imperfections might be made whole, yes, even the poor darn hen; and tears came into his eyes, which he relished, but he knew they had nothing to do with the deep contrition he was trying to recapture. Ye who do truly and earnestly repent you of your sins, he whispered almost aloud, and are in love and charity with your neighbors, draw near with faith and take this Holy Sacrament to your com-

fort, and make your humble confession to Almighty God, devoutly kneeling.

His heart opened. Almighty and everlasting
God, he prayed, Maker of all things, Judge of all
men (and he saw as in a wheeling rondure the
shining of all things, the shadows of all men), we
acknowledge and bewail our manifold sins and
wickednesses (and they manifolded themselves
upon the air between earth and heaven like falling
leaves and falling snow) which we from time to
time (and over and over, morning and noon and
waking in the night) most grievously have committed in thought (the wandering mind, the
lascivious image which even now flashed before
him), word (the words of obscenity and of cursing) and deed (the shame and the violence of the
hands) against Thy Divine Majesty (flung upward like so many arrows and so much filth
against the dying Son upon His Cross and the in-
vincible Father upon His Throne), provoking
most justly Thy wrath and indignation against
us (he bowed his head deeply, with eyes closed,
and the entire sky hardened into one spear driv-

ing downwards upon his bowed neck, yet Christ upon His Cross merely looked into his eyes without either wrath or indignation). We are heartily sorry for these our misdoings. The remembrance of them is grievous unto us (O yes it is surely grievous), the burden of them is (God, forgive me, forgive me, make them intolerable, intolerable), the burden of them is intolerable (it is, Lord, Lord God I want it to be), is intolerable. Have mercy upon us most merciful Father have mercy upon us (and he pressed his clasped hands tightly against his forehead), for Thy Son Our Lord Jesus Christ's sake forgive us all that is past (is past), and grant that we may ever hereafter serve Thee and please Thee in newness of life, to the honor and glory of Thy Name, Amen.

That we may ever hereafter. Ever hereafter. Serve Thee and please Thee. Serve Thee and please Thee in newness of life. Forgive us all that is past. All. Past. Ever hereafter, in newness of life. Serve Thee, and please Thee. To the honor and glory of Thy Name.

He was as peaceful and light almost, as if he

had just received Absolution. Keeping his eyes thinly closed, tilting his head quietly back, he could see the tender light of the candles against his eyelids, and he became aware once again of the strong fragrance of all the flowers. Dying, he whispered to himself. Soon now. For me and for all sinners. O sacred Head. He heard on his rose-mild blindness the infinitesimal flickering of the clock like those tiniest of thorns which cannot be taken out of the skin by thousands, by crown of piercing thorn. Opening his eyes just enough to see, looking through their rainbow flickering of little sharpness, sharp flames on the dark, thorn flames in thousands, each a thorn, a little sword, a tongue of fire, standing from pentecostal waxen foreheads; go ye unto all the world, a briarpatch of blessed fires, burning, just audibly crackling; no; the clock. Now pale flowers, round, in thousands, stared flatly among the thousands of sharp flames, as white and lonely on the humming gloom as organstops, gazed at too fixedly during a stupefying sermon, round and bright as wafers, consecrated Hosts, in the tiny burning and prickling of Time. He did not quite conceive of Time except as a power of measure upon the darkness, yet opened his eyes now and saw that it was almost twenty-five, twenty-three and a half, past four. The clock stood on the lowest step of the Altar. Its leather case was inlaid with silver wire almost as fine as hair, which outlined intricate flowers and leaves. It was his mother's, and it had been borrowed for use in the Lady Chapel, as it always was for this Thursday watch, because it was the most nearly silent clock on the place. Now that he looked at it he heard it the more clearly, a sound more avid and delicate than that of a kitten at its saucer, and now that he heard nothing else he saw nothing else except the face of the clock, hard, handless, staring white out of a shadow of trembling gold, like the great Host in a monstrance; and when once again he saw the hands, and the numbers, they showed that only two minutes of his watch remained. Could ye not watch with me one hour? Now he remembered the images and emotions into which he had awakened, so acutely, that they were al-

most his again; but now in some way they had
hardened, they stayed at some distance from him,
and he began to realize that during this entire
half-hour his mind had been wandering: there
had been scarcely one moment of prayer or of
realization. Hell of a saint I'd make, he said to
himself; and added with cold and level weary
self-disgust to the tally of the sins he must soon
confess, I swore in Lady Chapel in the presence
of the Blessed Sacrament. God be merciful unto
me a sinner, he whispered in his mind, crossing
himself.

Now for the first time he realized that his
knees were very sore. The small of his back
ached. When he moved, bending his back, shifting his knees, everything whirled hazily for a moment, then, with a kind of sliding or shunting like
the falling into plumb of a weighted curtain,
came clear and stayed still. I guess that was nearly
fainting, he thought, with satisfaction. He
searched the deep grooves in his knees along the
edge of the board and re-established them exactly

as they had been, and bore down on them to make them hurt the more, and he found that it hurt still more to keep his back completely straight and still, than to move it at all. The pain made him feel strong and reverent, and smiling he whispered silently to Jesus, "It's nothing to what You're doing." Our Father Who art in Heaven, he began; he knew now that he would stay another watch through.

Now it was half past four, but nobody moved. Nobody wants to be the first, he thought. No they're all praying, he told himself. I'm the only one noticed what time it is. Behind him he heard a sound of stealthy entering and of knees coming quietly to the floor. Now somebody will give up their place, he thought. It ought to be me.

Claude tilted his head to the other side and now Richard noticed the translucent lavender beads in his hands. He heard somebody stir and stand wearily up and he knew by the rustling starch that it was the Deaconess. She was in when I came. Been an hour. Maybe more. Quit keeping tabs, he told himself sharply. None of your busi-

ness. There was the sound of her going away and
the sound of another entering. Pray, he told himself. I ought to give my place. It was nearly
thirty-three minutes after. We beseech Thee O
Lord pour Thy Grace into our hearts, that——

The sacristy door opened and there was Lee
Allen. He looked more grave and tired than before and he avoided Richard's eyes with an aloof-
ness which abashed him. That as we have known
the Incarnation of Thy Son Jesus Christ through
the message of an Angel: Lee came silently to the
middle and genuflected; then from where he
stood, shifting the extinguishing cone in exact
rhythm, he put out seven shrunken candles to the
left and seven to the right. He genuflected again,
and leaned the tall snuffer into the corner, and
returned, and genuflected; then strode to the
Altar in a quiet and mastering way, reached delicately among the interlocked flowers, and up-
rooted with each hand a smoking seven-branched
candlestick. He genuflected once again and tiptoed out, shutting the door to softly with one
shoe. Smoke crinkled from each dark candle as

he went. There seemed to be scarcely fewer candles than before, there were so many. There would be others to change, five on each side; the rest were still tall enough. Through the message of an Angel, so by His Cross and Passion: he heard behind him the prudent raising of a window, and for the first time realized how suffocatingly hot it was, and that he was sweating. The sacristy door opened and there was George Fitzgerald. His eyes were softer and brighter with tiredness than before and his face was white and bright red in patches. He met Richard's eyes quietly and impersonally. He came to the middle and genuflected, and Richard could see that he was looking at all the flowers before he moved. Some still had strength and some were dying, and now he took two vases of those which were dying, unmeshing them with great care from among the others, and genuflected, and tiptoed out, shutting the door to softly with his shoe. Petals flaked away as he went. The living air touched the back of Richard's neck; now it even cooled his forehead; and now, rank on rank, the flames of the candles acknowledged the invading night; more petals fell. Upon the fragrance of fire and wax and fresh and dying flowers there stole the purity of water from a spring. Snaffling it desperately in an inept hand, somebody sneezed. Claude tilted his head back the first way and started his beads all over again. Richard heard the sound of bare feet withdrawing and knew that it must be Hobe and Jimmy. I haven't even said my prayers, he realized. I'm going to stay, he told himself. Give up your place, he told himself. You got no business hogging it. As much business as: you got no business thinking that either: as Claude with his head on one side and those beads. Give up your place. Come back. Kneel on the floor. The same person sneezed, more violently but better stifled. Claude, straightening his head, laid his beads down carefully, got up, stepped to the middle, genuflected, turned, looking like St. Sebastian, and went to the rear of the Chapel. Richard heard his careful sliding-shut of the window; the flames stood straight; Claude returned, and again began his beads at the beginning. Soul of Christ sanctify me, Richard began aimlessly; the sacristy door opened and there was Lee Allen.

Richard shut his eyes. O God forgive me that I can't do it right, he prayed. O God help me do it better now. Make me to love Thee and to know Thy suffering this day. For Jesus' sake Amen. He crossed himself meticulously and got to his feet; he was dizzy and for a moment his knees hurt very badly. He stepped out of the desk, genuflected, and turned, and all of a sudden he knew he would have to go out at least for a minute or two, he was much too tired to stay. When he turned to genuflect again at the door, Lee was lighting the second of the tall new candles.

The darkness was cool and stale. From where he stood beside the door of the Lady Chapel, looking back across the nave, he saw the spaced badges of blacker darkness where the Stations of the Cross hung veiled. Tall at his right shoulder, a Madonna stood, a blind black monolith. He walked silently towards the middle of the transept, and now he could see the white stops and keys of the organ. He stood at the center, facing the stripped Altar; sure that it ought not to be done, but in an obstinate and loyal reverence, he put down one knee and then both knees before the desolate shrine: until His coming again.

He bent his head deep towards the floor and heard his voice whisper slowly and fearfully within him the words which, he suspected, only a priest may utter without blasphemy: For in the night in which He was betrayed:

His skin crawled.

This is the night in which He is betrayed.

He felt the floor, bitter against his knees, and whispered aloud, "This is the night in which He is betrayed"; and with the whispering it no longer was, and he whispered within himself, He took bread, and brake it, and gave it unto His disciples, saying, Take, eat, this is my Body which is given for you; do this in remembrance of me.

He saw, and was himself, grown and vested, genuflecting, raising the consecrated Host, again genuflecting, while a bowed kneeling boy, who was also himself, shook the three bells.

Likewise after supper He took the cup, and when He had given thanks he blessed it, and gave it unto His disciples, saying, Drink ye all of this, for this is my Blood of the New Testament, which is shed for you and for many for the remission of sins. Do this as oft as ye shall drink it, in remembrance of me.

And with the words For this is my Blood of the New Testament, he knelt so deep in burden of blood that no priestly image entered him, and whispered again, Which is shed for you, and for many, for the remission of sins. And slowly one by one, while his hands lifted, the words stood up within his silence,

O Thou Lord God my Saviour: ("my Saviour," he whispered):

Look down on this Thy child.

Lord bless (he tried); O Lord lift up (he tried); O Lord forgive Thy child.

He could just see the empty Altar. There were no more words.

Do this as oft as ye shall drink it, in remembrance of me.

No more.

"Look down on this Thy child," he whispered aloud.

Now his knees hurt very badly.

"For Jesus' sake Amen," he whispered, crossing his breastbone with his thumb. He stood up.

If he went into the vestry they would say, What you doing up? They would tell him to go get on back to bed. Not mean about it because of the night it was but they would tell him all the same. Because it was the rule. Or maybe they wouldn't but if they did and he didn't go on back to bed it would be even worse than if they hadn't seen him. "I told him Father," he heard Lee Allen say in his serious hollow voice. "That's right Father," George Fitzgerald said, nodding soberly. And that was always worse when somebody had told you; Prefects. "What did you stay out for then?" "I dunno Father." "Course you know. Why did you stay out? Why did all of you stay out, Toole? You heard me tell you all to come straight back to bed." Where were they? He was suddenly scared. If they had gone back it would be even worse for him if he didn't go back too. "Where's Richard?" "I dunno Father." "Course you know, you all went together. Where is he?" "Honest Father *I* dunno. Last I seen him he was still in Lady Chapel." That ought to make it all right. Still in Lady Chapel. He was late but it was because he was praying. Can't whip anybody for that. "You know what the rule is." No. He'd say that to him, not them, him, at Council Meeting; they'd come back in time. "You know what I told you: come right on back to bed." "But I was staying a second watch Father. Ask Lee. Ask George if I wasn't." "I don't care what you were doing I told you to come straight back to bed and you didn't do any such thing. Now what have you got to say for yourself?" Or no, maybe he would look embarrassed and just mutter something about You see to it you do what you're told, and not punish him. Or no he would maybe look mad when he heard that about the second watch and say, "And you've got the nerve to use *that* for an excuse?" And yet the year before he had stayed a second watch and there had not been any trouble. But that year nobody had told him to come right on back to bed. That was the year three of the boys had never even showed up for the watch they signed for but went over to Lost Cove and got some whiskey.

If they'd gone on back he was in trouble already.

Breathing light, and the breathing shaken by his heart, with the greatest possible stealth he approached the vestry door and, stiffening beside the frame like an Indian scout, spied slopewise between the door and the jamb. George was carefully arranging wild azaleas in a Karo bucket. Lee was not there. Hobe squatted against the wall; Richard could see only his cheek, brown-orange in the light of the fiery mount of wax, which had grown much larger. Willard hung out all over the folding-chair; the quietly snoring head lay back and the blue chin was the highest part of it. Jimmy sat on the floor between his thighs; he looked very sleepy. Lee Allen came quickly out of the back passage at the far end and he seemed to look straight at Richard and Richard flinched away and froze, but it was clear by Lee's voice that he had not actually seen him. "Ought to wake up Burgy and send these kids to bed," he said. "They aren't doing any harm," George said. "*I* don't keer," Lee said, "but I don't want to get in no trouble either, you know what they told us." George said nothing for a little while and then he said, "Me neither," and after a little while he said, "I don't want you to get in trouble, count of me, Lee. You send them out if you want to. Don't let me hinder you." After thinking, Lee said, "Nobody hindern me." After a little he said, "Where's Sockertees?" which was one of Richard's nicknames, and Richard felt his breathing go thin. And Hobe said, exactly as Richard had fore-heard him, "Last I seen him he was still in Lady Chapel." "Well he ain't there now," Lee said. "Probly went on back to bed," George said. "No," he reflected, "we'd a heard him go out." "Crazy kid," Lee said. Richard tried to be sure whether this was said in affection or dislike, but so far as he could see it was neither, just an indifferent statement of fact. Dislike would almost have been better; and now he knew that he could not go in, right after Lee's saying that, and that although he felt very lonely, and suddenly wanted very much to be in there with them where no fuss was being made about not going to bed, he wanted still more not to be anywhere near them or anywhere near anybody. Crazy kid: crazy kid; yet he could not go away, for they might say more about him. He could hear George saying, "Oh, he's a good kid" or even just "Oh, he's all right," and it made everything much better, he could almost have gone in; but George didn't say anything of the kind, or anything at all, he just seemed to accept it as a fact everybody knew; and after a little Lee said, "I got to thin out them candles some if they're goana last through"; and George did not answer, and Lee said, "I thought there was a whole box more of them," and George said, "Not that I know of": and Lee did not answer, and George said, "If you thin out the candles some, maybe it'll give the flowers a chance, anyhow. I sure do hate to see dead flowers"; and suddenly, frightened because he was spying, Richard shrank as small against the wall as he could, for someone had come out of the Lady Chapel and now he could make out that it was Claude and realized thankfully, He sleeps in St. Joseph's, he'll go out the front. And sure enough Claude came to the middle as if to bow or genuflect and stood there a moment and then tossed his head upward to one side in a peculiar, saucy way, and turned his back on the Altar and walked back up the middle aisle and through the vestibule door; and after a moment Richard could hear the outside door; and then nothing; and after his breathing was quiet again, he crossed the transept without pausing to bow, and went back into the Lady Chapel.

The prayer-desks were all taken; he knelt at the rear on the bare floor and crossed himself, and closed his eyes, and bowed his head. Lord make my mind not to wander, he prayed, successfully driving from his mind Claude's impudent head. This is the last chance, he told himself. By leaning a little he could just see the clock. Already it was nearly quarter of. He felt fury against himself and subdued it, for it was evil. God be merciful unto me a sinner, he prayed, shutting his eyes again.

He waited carefully with his eyes closed but nothing came to him except his emptiness of soul and the pain of his knees and of his back. Hail Mary, he whispered to himself, and went through the prayer twice. He repeated five more Hail Marys rather rapidly and then three very slowly, trying to allow each word its full weight, and still there was nothing, not even through the words Pray for us sinners now and in the hour of our death. What's wrong with me, he wondered. He kept his eyes shut. Perhaps exactly because he had given his knees a rest, they now hurt worse than ever. Or it was because they were now on the flat floor, instead of braced against the edge of a board. The grooves where they had been against the board hurt badly, the bones just below the kneecaps hurt even worse. And within another minute or so, the small of his back ached worse than it had before. He bent over a little, and though that hurt his back in a new way, it also gave it a sort of rest. He let himself slacken down so that his buttocks sat on his heels, and that at least changed the pressure on the bones of his knees. He leaned forward so that his chest almost rested against his knees, and that helped his back. It'll just look like at Adoration, he reflected; and was ashamed of his hypocrisy. All the same, he thought, if it'll help me pray. Hail Mary, he prayed again. But still there was nothing. His heart was empty and his mind was idle, and he could not forget his discomfort.

He opened his eyes and looked around for a kneeling-pad and he saw one, skated against the baseboard, ahead of him and across the Chapel. He would have to get up and go in front of Julian to get it, and Julian was not using one. He hasn't been kneeling as long as I have, he reflected. What of it. He'll think I came in late. Just now. What of it. But the more he thought about it the more clearly he decided he would not go over and get the pad. If I can't say my prayers right, he told himself, why anyhow I can do this. He felt proudly and calmly vindictive against himself. Closely attentive to everything he was doing, he raised himself straight onto his knees and he straightened his spine so that his knees and the small of his back should hurt as much as possible, and he put the heels of his hands together, the fingers extended, edge to edge, tips touching, and the right thumb crossed over the left, as he had been taught when he was learning to be an acolyte. Ordinarily this strange and careful position of the hands embarrassed him, for it seemed sissy. Only a few of the servers kept to it; most of them, like Richard, simply folded their hands, and so did most of the priests; but now it seemed no more sissy than being on your knees in the first place. It was just the right way to hold your hands to pray, that was all. For all the aching in his knees and his back he was now even more clearly aware of his hands in this unaccustomed position, the palps of the fingers touching so lightly and competently, the locked thumbs, the cleanly hollow of shaded light within the palms; his hands felt full of goodness and quiet and they made him think of pictures of Cathedrals.

He tried to breathe so quietly that he could not feel his chest go in and out or even any air moving in his nostrils, and he gazed studiously at the monstrance, visualizing through the veil the spangling sunlike gold and the white center, and upon that center Christ Crucified, Whom he saw first in metal and then in wood and then in flesh; but he began to wonder whether these efforts at visualization were not mere tricks and temptations of emptiness, for still he was empty of prayer and of feeling. Now that he forbade himself images and dwelt within the discipline of his body his knees and his back began to hurt worse than ever and he began to think with quiet and increasing amazement of young men, boys really, hardly older than he was, not much older than George anyway, who knelt like this on Chapel stone the whole night through in prayer and vigil, their weapons and armor blessed and waiting, soberly shining in the lambent gloom, before the Mass and the Communion and before the greatest moment of their lives when their King touched the flat of the sword to the shoulder and the young man stood up and was assisted in putting upon himself the whole armor of God and rode forth into the glittering meadows of daybreak for the first time a knight, a knight errant, seeking whatever wrong God might send him to set right, whatever tests of valor and chastity the huge world might hold in ambush for him. O but I can do better than this, he exclaimed to himself in self-contempt; and he thought with envy and reverence of the early time which had belonged to those shining young men, and he pressed down with all his strength and weight, first on one knee and then on the other, so that it was hard not to cry out, and he held his back still more rigidly upright, and he was pleased to find that now, by the way he held his hands out, even his arms ached, deep into the shoulders. But it's so little to do! he thought, imagining the first, living Crucifix; and he did his best to imagine one hand, against splintery wood, and the point of a spike against the center of the open hand, and a great hammer, and the spike being driven through, breaking a bone, tight into the wood so that the head was all buried in the flesh and the splintered bone, and then to be able to say, *Father forgive them for they know not what they do.* And that's just one hand, he reminded himself. How about both hands. And both feet. Specially both feet crossed on each other and one spike through both insteps. How about when they raise up the Cross with you on it and drop it deep into the hole they dug for it! And imagining that moment he felt a tearing spasm of anguish in the center of each palm and with an instant dazzling of amazed delight, remembering pictures of great saints, shouted within himself, *I've got the Wounds!* and even as he caught himself opening his palms and his eyes to peer and see if this were so he realized that once again this night, and even more blasphemously and absurdly than before, he had sinned in the proud imagination of his heart. *O my God*, his heart moaned, *O my God! My God how can You forgive me!* I'll have to confess it, he realized. I can't. Not this. How can I confess *this!*

The thing he had most dreaded to confess before, an impure act which in its elaborateness had seemed merely the more exciting in the doing and which was so nearly unbearable to specify to another, and a priest at that, that he had gravely considered the risk to his soul of merely generalizing it: beside this new enormity—and twice over in one night, and both times in the Presence —beside this, that ugly and humiliating lustfulness seemed almost easy to tell of. But I'll tell it all the same, he told himself grimly. Because if I don't I'm in mortal sin. No I'll tell it because I did it and I hate to so much, and I don't care who it is I have to tell it to either, I won't dodge whoever it turns out to be and wait for another, not even if it's Father McPhetridge. I'll tell the whole thing just the way it happened—way I thought it happened, that is. I'll tell it all right. Because I've got to.

He looked proudly at the monstrance and felt strength and well-being stand up straight inside him, and self-esteem as well; for it began to occur

to him that not many people would even know
this for the terrible sin it was, or would feel a
contrition so deep, or would have the courage
truly and fully, in all of its awful shamefulness,
to confess it: and again the strength and the self-
esteem fell from him and he was aghast in the
knowledge that still again in this pride and complacency he had sinned and must still again confess; and again that in recognizing this newest sin
as swiftly as it arose, and in repenting it and determining to confess it as well, he had in a sense
balanced the offense and restored his well-being
and his self-esteem; and again in that there was
evil, and again in the repenting of it there was
good and evil as well, until it began to seem as if
he were tempted into eternal wrong by rightness
itself or even the mere desire for rightness and as
if he were trapped between them, good and evil,
as if they were mirrors laid face to face as he had
often wished he could see mirrors, truly reflecting
and extending each other forever upon the darkness their meeting, their facing, created, and he
in the dark middle between them, and there was

no true good and no true safety in any effort he
might ever make to realize or repent a wrong but
only a new temptation which his very soul itself
seemed powerless to resist; for was not this sense
of peace, of strength, of well-being, itself a sin?
Yet how else could a forgiven or forgivable soul
possibly feel, or a soul in true contrition or self-
punishment? I'm a fool to even try, he groaned
to himself, and he felt contempt for every moment of well-being he could recall, which had
come of the goodness of a thought or word or
deed. *Everything* goes wrong, he realized. Everything anyone can ever do for himself goes wrong.
Only His Mercy. That's what He died for. That's
what He's dying for today. Only His Mercy can
be any help. Nothing anyone can do but pray.
O God, he prayed, be *merciful* unto *me, a sinner*.
Let me not feel good when I am good. *If* I am
good. Let me just try to be good, don't let me
feel good. Don't let me even *know* if I'm good.
Just let me try. And in this humility, aware that
it was of a true and pure kind which was new to
him, he felt a flash of relief, well-being, pride:

and tightening his shut eyes, cried out in despair within himself, *There it is again! O God make it go away. Make it not mean anything. O God what I can't help, please forgive it.* He wanted to put himself down on his face on the floor. "*All my trust I put in Thee,*" he whispered aloud and, aware that he had whispered aloud, opened his eyes in the fear that he had been noticed. Nobody seemed to have noticed. Now Jimmy and Hobe were kneeling a little ahead of him. He found that he was drenched with sweat and as short of breath as if he had been running. He felt weak and quiet. The burden of them is intolerable. He could feel the words sincerely and quietly now yet at the same time they meant nothing to him. All my trust I put in Thee, he repeated silently. O let me not fail Thee.

Tonight.
This very night.
For in the night in which He was betrayed.
Now fragments of his first moment awake returned but now they were dry and tired like dead

leaves, as dry and tired as he was. He tried to realize what it all meant. But all that he could realize was dry and tired like the tired dry fire of the candles.

He came into the world to be with us and save us, and this is what happened. This is what it all came to.

The light shineth in darkness and the darkness comprehended it not.

He came unto His own and His own received Him not.

So there He was just sitting there waiting. Just waiting to die.

Words stirred and stood up inside him which lifted his heart: But as many as received Him, to them gave He power to become the sons of God.

And the Word was made Flesh and dwelt among us:

He closed his eyes and bowed his head.

Flesh.

All for us.

All his suffering for all of us.

He remembered the terrible thing his uncle

had said: "Well who *asked* him to die for me? *I*
didn't. He needn't try and collect on the debt,"
he had said, "because there's no debt, far's I'm
concerned." Nearly always when he thought of
this Richard was shocked almost into awe of such
blasphemy; and some few times when some priest
or his mother was insisting what we all owe Jesus
he had been tempted to wonder, wasn't it maybe
really so, for it was a fact; Jesus had done it without anybody asking Him to: but now it seemed
neither blasphemous nor persuasive but only
empty and idle and cruel and as he thought of it
he could see the man of whom it had been said,
sitting very quietly on a stool or maybe a bench
among the iron-breasted helmeted soldiers while
they hit him and spat in his face and mocked him.
Nobody could come near him or help him or
even speak a word of love or thanks or comfort
to him now. He could see him only as if he spied
down on what was happening through a cellar
window and it would be torture and death to dare
to even try to get in, and no use could come of it,
even if he did. The way, maybe, Peter had stayed.

All of Peter's betraying and cowardliness was over and done with now. Nothing could ever wipe out for him what he had done. He wasn't even crying any more because he couldn't even cry any more. He was just hiding around on the outskirts, spying through the window. He was afraid to show himself and he couldn't stand to go away. He must wish he was dead.

Judas, by now, had he hanged himself? Richard couldn't remember for sure when. But if he hadn't yet, that was all there was left for him to do. That was all he was thinking about all the rest of this night, all that was left of his life. I want to die. O I want to be dead. I can't be dead soon enough to suit me. Judas didn't feel contrition, Father Weiler said, he felt remorse. Probably he couldn't cry like Peter. Just terrible cold remorse, as cold and bitter as the sound of the word. Remorse is very different from contrition; a deadly sin. A mortal sin is a sin that cuts us off from God. With remorse you don't feel sorry like contrition, you feel, well you just feel remorse, that's all.

These were just the dead hours. The hours between. They must be the worst hours of all for Jesus and for everyone who loved Him. No more doubt now. No more praying to God the Father, if this Cup can be taken from me: that's over long ago. It can't. That's all. No more judgment, standing trial, answering fool questions. He's already been sentenced to die. He belongs to the Law. Now just the time between. So tired. No sleep all this night. Waiting, getting Himself ready inside, while they mock and sneer and holler at him, and spit in his face, and crown him with thorns, and put the reed in his hand for a scepter, just waiting through the rest of the long night, just getting ready to die, while the night slowly turns into morning, and it's the last morning of all. To suffer so he will cry out, *My God, my God, why hast Thou forsaken me?* And then die. *It is finished.* And then die. And meekly bowing down His head, He gave up the ghost. And then (Richard could remember in advance) the stunned and strange peacefulness, throughout that afternoon and night and through all the next day, and the quiet, almost secret lighting of the tremendous candle in the beginning of the dusk of Holy Saturday, everything still going as if on tiptoe, and then in the first light of morning, the stillest and most wonderful moment of the year, the quietly spoken and simple Mass: "He is risen." And then the rich midmorning and blinding blaze of Easter. *'Tis the Spring of Souls today, Christ hath burst His prison, and from three days' sleep in Death, like a Sun hath risen.*

But not yet. That is still not known though at the same time it *is* known. We are all in most solemn sorrow and grief and mourning. We know a secret far inside ourselves but we don't dare tell it, even to ourselves. We don't dare to quite believe it will ever really happen again until it really happens again. Until His coming again. For in the night in which He was betrayed. It has happened over nineteen hundred times now and yet it has never happened before. Not yet. And we don't know if it ever can. Never dreamed it could. Can.

Not yet. Now is just the dead time between and he is waiting. This is his last night and his last daybreak begins soon now. Before this day is over he will be dead.

My Jesus, he whispered, clasping his hands strongly; his throat contracted.

O Saviour of the World Who by Thy Cross and Precious Blood hast redee——

O you are dying my dear Lord for me, his soul whispered, wondering, weeping. For *me*, and I can't do anything for you. I can't even comfort you, or speak to you, or thank you. O my Lord Jesus I can thank you. I can think about you. I can try to know what it is you are going through for me. For me and for all sinners. I can know that every sin I do big or no matter how little is a thorn or a nail or the blow of the hammer or even just a fly that teases and hurts you in your blood, crawling and tickling and sipping and eating at you in the hot day on the Cross with you unable to brush him away or even to move, and every good thing, or true thankfulness or thought of love must make it anyway a little less terrible to suffer. My Lord I love Thee. My Lord I grieve for Thee. My dear Lord I adore Thee. My poor

Lord I wish I could suffer for Thee. My Lord I thank Thee. Lord have mercy upon me. Christ have mercy upon me. Lord have mercy upon me.

He opened his eyes in quiet wonder. It was indeed to him the very day. Not just a day in remembrance, but the day. There stood His consecrated Body, veiled among fire and flowers, but also living, in the flesh, on this very morning, at this very moment, He was waiting; and He was now within His last hours.

He won't see the sun go down today.

He looked at all the lights, spearing, aspiring, among the dying flowers. Knobbled and fluted with their own spillings, the candles stood like sheaves; some, bent by the heat, bowed over like winter saplings. Almost all the flowers hung their exhausted faces. They were so shrunken and disheveled now that he could see clearly among them the many shapes and sizes of the vessels which held them, the professional vases and ewers and jars, and the tumblers and tin cans from the poor cabins out the Mountain. He could just hear the clock. Tonight, he whispered, watching that devastation. This night. This minute. He leaned, and looked at the clock. It was one minute after five. Something troubled him which he had done or had left undone, some failure of the soul or default of the heart which he could not now quite remember or was it perhaps foresee; he was empty and idle, in some way he had failed. Yet he was also filled to overflowing with a reverent and marveling peace and thankfulness. My cup runneth over, something whispered within him, yet what he saw in his mind's eye was a dry chalice, an empty Grail. No more I could do, he reflected, if I stayed all night. No more. No use: and he continued merely to look without thought at the emblazoned ruin. "Goodbye," something whispered from incalculably deep within him. *O goodbye, goodbye,* his heart replied. A strange and happy sorrow filled him. *It is finished,* his soul whispered. He looked at the humbled backs ahead of him and prayed: The peace of God which passeth all understanding keep our hearts and minds in the knowledge and love of God, and of His Son Jesus Christ. And the blessing of God Almighty, the Father, the Son and the Holy Ghost, be amongst us and remain with us always.

He opened his eyes; and it was all as was before. Of course it was. He was light and uneasy and at peace within. There was nothing to do or think or say.

He signed himself carefully with the Cross, got up, genuflected, and left the Chapel; just inside the north door, he took off his shoes. Hobe and Jimmy came up behind him and they took off their shoes too.

THE
MORNING WATCH

III

THEY WALKED DOWN the sandstone steps into an air so different from the striving candles and the expiring flowers that they were stopped flatfooted on the gravel. Morning had not yet begun but the night was nearly over. The gravel took all the light there was in the perishing darkness and shed it upward, and in the darkness among the trees below the outbuildings a blossoming dogwood flawed like winter breath. In the untouchable silence such a wave of energy swept upward through their bare feet and their three bodies into the sky that they were shaken as if a ghost had touched them. Sharply and almost silently, Hobe laughed.

They looked at the last tired stars and·at the dark windows of their dormitory and then wondered what their punishment would be.

"S - - t fahr," Hobe said. "Can't even pray, what the f - - - *kin* ye do!"

Maybe, Richard reflected, they wouldn't say anything. Couldn't be a better excuse than praying. In brainless exaltation he flexed the soles of his feet against the ground. What of it if they do.

Rustily, so far down back of them across the fields they could scarcely hear him, a rooster crowed.

"Let's get the rackets," Richard said.

They took it as naturally as if one of them had said it.

"They'd catch us sure," Jimmy said.

"Hell we keer," Hobe said. "Tan our asses anyhow, now."

Creakily, a little nearer, but very faint, a second rooster answered.

Might not, Richard thought; not *anyhow*. What if they do.

"Let's go to the Sand Cut," Hobe said.

"Freeze yer balls off," Jimmy said.

"Sun-up, time we git thur," Hobe said.

Proud, fierce behind the cook's house, the cry of a third rooster shining sprang, speared, vibrated as gaily and teasingly in the centers of their flesh as a jews-harp.

"Come on," Richard said, and started walking rapidly across the pale gravel.

He was surprised that he had spoken and the more surprised to hear them following. How they do it, he thought, stepping along not quite steadily in silent uneasy elation; all there is to it. He led them down past the cook's house.

Pride, he realized; a mortal sin. How do I confess that?

Through the veering wire net he saw, black in the faintness, how the big rooster darted his vigilant head and shuffled his plumage: in the silence before daylight a priest, vesting himself for Mass. Something heavy struck and the whole body splayed, and chuckled with terror; the coward's wives gabbled along their roost.

Richard felt as if he had been hit in the stomach.

I'm scared of both of them, he reflected, specially Hobe, and they know it whenever they want to.

And bigger than either of them, he forced himself to recognize.

Younger. Big for his age that's why I'm clumsy and soft.

Bigger all the same.

Maybe that makes up for the Pride, he thought, as they walked past the bruising foulness of the backhouse.

Privately, safe ahead of them, he struck his breast.

Nothing makes up for anything. Confess you thought it did.

He tried to imagine how to confess it. I have sinned the sin of Pride and some other sin I don't know the name of. I was proud because when I said let's go to the Sand Cut (and it wasn't even me that thought of it first) they came along just as if one of them had said it and all of a sudden I knew that all you have to do is say something and go ahead yourself without waiting and they'll do it. Then something happened that made me know I was scared of them and I admitted to myself I'm : yellow : and then I thought maybe because I made myself admit that, why then I wouldn't have to confess I was proud before. I thought it made up for it.

He tried to imagine the priests to whom he would confess this. Father McPhetridge, Father Whitman, Father Weiler, Father Ogle, Father Fish. Unless maybe if he got Father Fish but even if you tried to dodge and choose which was probably a sin why you couldn't ever tell for sure who you'd get. The others would just think he was crazy or something. Crazy kid. Or trying to get credit. And maybe he would be.

What you say in Confession they never tell because if they do they go straight to Hell. But whoever you confess to, he knows all the same. And if he knows you honestly are trying hard to be good he gives you credit afterwards too, that you sin if you try to get, he can't help himself. And if he thinks you're just trying to get credit why everytime he looks at you from then on you know what he thinks of you.

If he really thought you were, though, probably he wouldn't give you Absolution.

If you know it's a sin why you've got to confess it, no matter what he thinks.

The ferment of the hogpen, deepest of blacks and heaviest of oils, so stuffed and enriched their nostrils that as one they slowed against the fence and looked in. Small as the light was, on all its edges the chopped muck shone like coal. Jimmy slid his hand inside his overalls against his naked body; becoming aware of what he had done, he thoughtfully withdrew it. Straining to see into the darkness of the shed they could just discern the close-lying egglike forms of the hogs.

"Oink: oink," Hobe grunted, in a voice so deep that Richard was surprised.

Crooomphth, a sleeping hog replied.

They crossed the stile and struck into the

woods, using their unhardened feet somewhat delicately along the familiar path. It was as thrilling cold and as vague and silent here as leaving a hot morning and stepping into a springhouse, and the smell of dead leaves and decaying wood and of the arising year was as keen as the coldness. A dogwood dilated ahead of them, each separate blossom enlarging like an eye, and swung behind, and deeply retired among the black trees ahead they could see the shining of others in the first light, triumphal and sad, lonesome as nebulae; likewise blind clumps of unawakened laurel; and now as the light became adequate they saw that the floor of the woods was still the leathery color of last year's leaves, meagerly stitched with green. In the deeper distances the woods were neutral as a photograph, as they had been all winter, but nearer by, the trunks of the trees were no longer black. Some were blackish, some were brownish, some were gray and gray green and silver brown and silver green and now the forms and varieties of bark, rugged, mosaic, deeply ribbed and satin sleek, knobbled like lepers and fluted like columns

of a temple, became entirely distinct. Some of the
twigs looked still as dark and fragile as the middle
of winter, many were knobbled and pimpled and
swollen as if they were about to break open
and bleed, and many were the color of bronze and
some were the color of blood; on some there were
little buds like the nubbins of young deer and on
others new leaves as neatly fledged as the feather-
ing ought to be for the arrows Richard had never
been able to make perfectly. They could see a
long way into the woods as the morning cleared
and everywhere underfoot this leather laid its flat
musing waves and everywhere among the retreat-
ing trees strayed sober clouds of evergreen and
mild clouds of blossom and the dreaming laurels,
and everywhere, as deep into the stunned woods
as they could see, layer above unwavering layer,
the young leaves led like open shale; while, against
their walking, apostolically, the trees turned. The
path among these winding, dancing trees, new to
them since late fall, was supple underfoot, the
droning trees against which they laid or slapped
their hands felt as alive as the flanks of horses, the

air was all one listening joy. While they approached the clearing each held in mind a festival imagination of the plum tree, but it hung black, all crazed elbows, in the widened light. From somewhere, however, the fallen silvers of the ruined house it seemed, they were pursued by the chiding, familiar song of an ambushed bird whose kind they did not know; and at the far side of the clearing Richard stopped short and the others passed him: for here, abject against sharp bark, he found a locust shell, transparent silver breathed with gold, the whole back split, the hard claws, its only remaining strength, so clenched into the bark that it was only with care and gentleness that he was able to detach the shell without destroying it.

It was as if air had been tightened into substance; only by touch and sight, not at all by weight, could he know he held it. He held it in his cupped hand and looked at the hunched, cloven back, turned it over with one fingertip and examined the brutally elaborate structure of the legs and the little talons. He tested: they

could pierce a finger. He turned it again and held
it near his eyes: the eyes looked into his. Yet even
the eyes were there, blind silver globes which had
so perfectly contained the living eyes: even the
small rudimentary face in its convulsed and fierce
expression, the face of a human embryo, he could
remember the engraving in a book of his grandfather's, a paroxysm of armor, frowning, scowl-
ing, glaring, very serious, angry, remote, dead, a
devil, older, stranger than devils, as early, ancient
of days, primordial, as trilobites. Dinosaurs
heaved and strove; a pterodactyl, cold-winged,
skated on miasmic air, ferns sprang, to make coal
in these very coves, more huge than the grandest
chestnuts. Silurian, Mesozoic, Protozoic, Jurassic,
all the planet one featureless and smoky marsh,
Crowns, Thrones, Dominions, Principalities,
Archaeozoic, through all ranks and kingdoms, to
the central height, armed in the radiant cruelty of
immortal patience, Ages and Angels marched
clanging in his soul.

When did he come out? Just now? Just this

spring? Or has he stayed all winter? And that would mean all fall and summer before.

I'd have seen him; last fall; last spring.

If he was there all the time and I didn't before, how come I saw him now?

All winter. All year. Or just since the first warm weather. Or just now before I found him.

That whole split back. Bet it doesn't hurt any worse than that to be crucified.

He crossed himself.

He sure did hold on hard.

He tried to imagine gripping hard enough that he broke his back wide open and pulled himself out of each leg and arm and finger and toe so cleanly and completely that the exact shape would be left intact.

With veneration, talon by talon, he re-established the shell in its grip against the rigid bark.

By the time he caught up with Hobe and Jimmy they were almost to the railroad track.

At the far end of the break in the woods along the far side of the track they saw the weathered oak tower and soon, walking more briskly along

the ties, the relics of machinery and the dead cones
of putty-colored sand and the wrinkled sandstone
and, at length, the sullen water itself, untouched
in all these cold months. There were black slits
along the sides of the tower where planks had
fallen during the winter. The water was motion-
less and almost black. The whole place, familiar
as it was, was deadly still, and seemed not at all
to welcome them. As they left the track to round
the near end of the Sand Cut there was a scuttling
among the reddened brambles but although they
went as fast as they could on their soft feet and
threw rocks where the brambles twitched with
noise they got no glimpse of whatever it was, and
soon the scuttling stopped.

Now that they had stopped walking and stood
in the brightened silence of the open light the day
began to look practical; they realized how chilly
the air still was, even here out of the woods, and
how bitter the water looked, and they no longer
felt like going in. But none of them was willing
to admit this frankly even to himself, and it was
only after they stripped that they became openly

hesitant. They took care not to shiver more visibly than they could help or to appear to dawdle, either, but they did all dawdle, and they found that they were looking at each other, in this unhabitual place and hesitant quietness, with more interest than in the dormitory. Although Jimmy was the smallest of the three in every other way, his was much the biggest and during the winter he had grown more hair than Richard had realized up to now. Hobe still didn't have much but then he was said to be part Indian so of course he wouldn't, yet, and probably never would have a lot. What he did have was dark, though, and showed up well against his dark skin, whereas Richard's was so light and there was so little of it that he realized it could probably not be seen at all, farther away than his own eyes. He suspected, however, that his was really the biggest, because it looked as if Jimmy had at least half a hard-up. Jimmy looked comfortable in his supremacy whether it was real or not (he certainly had more hair, anyhow, there wasn't any getting around that) and seemed to feel none of the embarrass-

ment which Richard always felt acutely if he
was seen with even a little bit of a hard-up. He
turned partly away, though, in honor of Good
Friday, and for the same reason he and Richard
glanced at each other with even less candor than
they would have at any other time, and Richard
the more uneasily crossed and uncrossed his hands
in front of himself. Only Hobe, of any boy
Richard knew, never concealed his own body or
his interest in another, and even now, Good Friday seemed to mean nothing to him. He looked
at them, and watched them look at him, with a
coolness which seemed almost amused. He
urinated a few drops onto his belly and rubbed it
in with the palm of his hand, against cramps. He
made no gesture of covering himself and grabbed
his testicles with one hand only at the instant he
grabbed his nose with the other to leap with a
spangling splash into the water.

He bounced up with an incredulous strangling
yell and began a frenzied dogpaddle and both of
them knew the water must be even colder than
they had thought, and that there was no longer

any chance of holding back. Jimmy went in feet first; Richard dove. The iron water distended enormously just beneath him and for an instant, knowing the brutal shock and the pain to which he had now inescapably committed himself, he felt the fatal exhilaration of a falling dream and had just time to dedicate within himself *for Thee!* in a silent shout as deafening bright as a smiting of cymbals; then plunged into the smashing cold. Still crying *for Thee* within his ringing head, he slanted his hands to dive as deep as he could go and, though his eyes were open, could see nothing of the steep sandstone along which his hands guided him, but only the stifled effulgence of light above. It was so much colder than he had been able to imagine that in the first moment he had felt almost unconscious, but the diver's reflex had locked his breath and now that he searched from ledge to ledge downward along the much colder bottom there sprang throughout his flesh such an ardent and serene energy that he was aware of the entire surface of his body as if it were fire, and every muscle seemed to feel its own

135

exact shape and weight, and he wished that he need never come up and lay against the deepest trench of the bottom, his belly foundering in ooze, his eyes shut, staying his hands on rocks. He lifted his face free of the ooze and cautiously opened his eyes; he could feel, more clearly than be sure he saw, the light which enlarged above him. He turned his head and looked up sidelong; there it was, a pure, heavy slab of still light which by imperceptible degrees shaded downward into most deadly darkness. His chest and his head began to knock, it became harder with every pulse to hold onto the rocks. O Lord let me suffer with Thee this day, he prayed, his lungs about to burst; and took hold more firmly. You got no right, his own voice silently told him, you got no right. No right; but still he fought off his need for air, filling his cheeks with the exhausted air from his lungs and taking it down again in the smallest possible gulps. His head was beating and ringing so fiercely that he could scarcely hear the fragments of his own efforts to dedicate and to reprove himself but blindly, with the last of his strength, held himself down. Then he knew that he had stayed down too long; too deep; he could not possibly reach the air in time. Good. That's fine. *For Thee!* he groaned. *No right! Get out!* he shouted silently. But even before he could command it or fully decide to command it his body was working for him; his feet braced against a ledge, his knees bent, and he leapt upward through the brightening water with more strength than he had realized he had left although the water seemed interminably tall above him and he knew still that he would never reach the surface in time and cried out to himself, *I didn't have the nerve!* and, *Anyhow I tried*, meaning at once that he had tried to stay down too long as an act of devotion and that he had tried to save himself from the deadliest of sins; and broke the surface in time, head back, gasping, feebly treading water, watching the streaming bruise-colored clamorous and silent whirling of the world and taking in air so deeply that his lungs felt as if they were tearing; and soon the world became stable and all of the coloring and discoloration cleared and stood

up strongly through the top of the woods across
the tracks and he could realize that except for the
remote voices of the two boys and the still more
remote voice of a bird the world itself was delicately silent and all the noise was within his own
head and was rapidly dying: all that he saw still
twitched with his pulse and out of the woods,
beating like a heart, the sun stood up.

His teeth still ached at their roots and although
he clenched them to keep from chattering his
chin trembled like a rabbit's nose and his breath
came out shakily in many small pieces as of glass
or ice. From its surface down to about his waist,
the water seemed surprisingly warm, but from
waist to knees it was grimly cold, and his stony
feet trod a mortal bleakness of cold and dark to
which he was thankfully sure now that he would
never go down again. Yet except for his feet,
which no longer seemed to belong to him, his
body still blazed with pleasure in its existence, and
it was no longer urgent and rigid but almost
sleepy. He slid his slick hands along his ribs and
his sides and found that in his sex he was as tightly

shrunken as if he were a baby. I could have died, he realized almost casually. *Here I am!* his enchanted body sang. I could be dead right now, he reflected in sleepy awe. *Here I am!* Now that he had his breath and was quiet he no longer tried to control the rattling of his teeth but hung standing in the water, his head so turned from the others that they might not see the silent unexpected tears and, drowsily trying to make himself aware of the suffering to which at this moment Jesus was submitting Himself, crying for tenderness and thankful wonder, gazed steadily into the beating sun.

But staying still so long, coldness at length overcame him, and after swimming as fast as he could twice up and down the length of the quarry, he stumbled out.

He had all but forgotten them; they were already drying themselves with their shirts. Hobe's body was purplish; Jimmy looked as if he had been caught in a blue net.

"What you trine to do?" Hobe asked. "Drownd yourself?"

"I was just swimming under water."

"I was damn near ready to dive in after you," Jimmy said, "when you come up."

"We began to think you was drownded," Hobe said.

"No, I was all right," Richard said. He reached for his shirt. *"Heyy!"* he shouted.

Steering, serenely, his sutured brow, the sum of those several thrusting curves which seemed not of themselves to exert strength but merely to drink and send backward through them the energies of the guiding head they guided, a snake more splendid than Richard had ever seen before was just achieving a sandstone ledge and the first heat of the risen sun. In every wheaten scale and in all his barbaric patterning he was new and clear as gems, so gallant and sporting against the dun, he dazzled, and seeing him, Richard was acutely aware how sensitive, proud and tired he must be in his whole body, for it was clear that he had just struggled out of his old skin and was with his first return of strength venturing his new one. His style and brightness, his princely elegance,

the coldness of his eye and the knifelike coldness
and sweetness of his continuously altering line,
his cold pride in his new magnificence, were not
at the first in the least dismayed, not even by Richard's shout; only the little tongue, to Richard's
almost worshiping delight and awe, sped like a
thready horn of smoke, the eye seemed to meet
Richard's and become colder and still more
haughty, and the vitality of his elegance advanced
him still further along the stone: so that for a few
seconds Richard saw perfected before him, royal-
ly dangerous and to be adored and to be feared,
all that is alien in nature and in beauty: and stood
becharmed. But as the others ran up, within an
instant so swift that it was impossible to see just
what transpired among those curves of liquid
paroxysm, with a chilly rasping against stone
which excited Richard as nothing he had ever
heard before had excited him, drawing a stripe of
coldness down his spine, the snake reversed direc-
tion and slipped rapidly between the ankles of
briars and beneath fallen leaves, his brilliance a
constant betrayal. The others were shouting and

Jimmy shoved a stick under the snake and flipped him so expertly that for a couple of seconds he sailed on the air in a convulsion of escape, a fluid hieroglyph, and landed on open rock in a humiliating flash of ivory belly before he righted himself and with oily fleetness made once more for the bushes. But now Hobe reared up a rock so heavy he could lift it only clumsily, high above his reeling head; and Richard, standing just behind him, felt himself reach towards the rock to pull it backwards out of his hands. But even as his own hand lifted forward he became aware of Jimmy's astounded eye on him, and thus became aware of what he was doing and caught himself, realizing that they would never understand why he did it, that they would be angry with him and rightly so and might even be mad enough to jump on him; and becoming thus aware, became aware also that it was not only his habit of gentleness to animals which made him want to spare the snake, but something new in him which he could not understand, about which he was profoundly uneasy. These several kinds of awareness came over him with terrible speed and transfixed him into the slowness of a dream, so that the fraction of a second froze the high rock, the incredulous bystander, the bemused hand, and seemed to last almost interminably, while he strove to stay his hand and to set it free. But it was after all only an instant, and before he could bring himself out of this hesitation, Hobe brought the rock crashing down against rock and against one arc of the veering snake which, angled like a broken whip, continued uselessly to thrust energy through its ruptured body, its eyes terrible, its tongue so busy that its speed made the shadow of a blossom. Jimmy hurried up with his stick and beat at its head but the head was still alert to dodge under his blows. Richard felt for a moment as if he had just finished retching. Then he picked up a small rock and yelling "*Get out of the way*," squatted beside the snake and pounded at its head. The head lashed about his fist like summer lightning as he pounded and in the darkness of his violence the question darted, over and over, *is he poison? is he poison?* but he cared only for one thing, to put as quick an end as he could to all this terrible, ruined, futile writing and unkillable defiance, and at length he struck and dazed, and struck and missed, and struck and broke the head which nevertheless lifted senilely, the tongue flittering and the one remaining eye entering his own eye like a needle; and again, and the head lay smashed and shifting among its debris; and again, and it was flattened against the stone, though still the body, even out beyond the earlier wound, lashed, lay resting, trembled, lashed.

As he watched this trembling twitching, desperately wishing that he could so crush the snake that it would never move again, he realized that it would not die until sundown, and even as he realized this he heard Hobe say it and became aware, through something quiet in Hobe's voice and through Jimmy's shyness, that they respected him; that in putting his bare hand within range of that clever head and in killing so recklessly and with such brutality, he had lost their contempt and could belong among them if he wanted to. He looked coldly at his trembling hand: bloody at the knuckles and laced with slime, which seemed to itch and to burn as it dried, it still held the rock.

"Better warsh that stuff off," Hobe said. "Git in your blood: *boy!*"

He still squatted, looking at his hand and wondering. In their good opinion, and in the rugged feeling of the hand itself and its ferocious moisture, he began to feel that he had been brave in a way he had never been brave before and he wanted the hand to clear gradually and naturally, the way the smudge clears from the forehead on Ash Wednesday. He could not be sure, in its pristine skin, what kind of snake this was, and the head was wrecked beyond any hope of determining whether it had the coffin shape, or venomous fangs. But it was not a rattler, nor was it likely a copperhead, nor was it striped like a moccasin, so that he had to doubt whether, after all, it had been poisonous. If it had not been poisonous he had not been brave; and if it had not been poisonous he was sorry he had killed it or even been fool enough to yell so the others would see it and so

automatically kill it, for he had for a long while
been fascinated by snakes and had felt that the
harmless ones ought to be let alone, as few people
let them alone. He was aware that Hobe had
spoken and that he had given no kind of answer,
and this made him uneasy. He wanted very much
to taste the slime; but they were watching. He
turned up the rock and looked at it; the slime and
breakage of the snake caught the whitening sunlight like mica. He slammed the rock into the
middle of the water (just about where I dove in,
he realized upon reflection) and clambered cautiously down to the edge and thrust his hand into
the cold water and up to the elbow, beating
quietly in the brilliant cold, and watched it in the
water; the veins stood out on his forearm almost
like a man. He decided that he would only sub-
merge his hand, not wash it, no matter what
Hobe advised. But Hobe said nothing.

They dressed thoughtfully and they had very
little to say; now that they were on their way
back there wasn't much to think about except the
trouble which waited for them. There would

have been trouble even if they had come straight back from Chapel, for they had outstayed the watch they had signed for by a long time. But they began to realize now that it would not have been as bad as it was bound to be now; maybe they'd even have been let off. If they had gotten back to bed at any time before daylight it wouldn't have been as bad as it would be now. If they had come in just while the sun was rising it would have been bad but not as bad as this. Now it was broad daylight and brighter every minute, and with every minute longer now that they stayed away they were in for worse trouble. They might be kept on bounds, they might have to pull stumps or clean out the pit of the back-house, they might be whipped, they might even not be let go on the Easter Monday picnic and they had planned to go clear to Wet Cave which had never yet been fully explored, and find new passages and, if possible, a new and secret entrance. There was no telling what, for the worst of it was that they had gone against a strict rule so conspicuously on Good Friday, and by taking advantage of a religious event, and there was no way of imagining how much more serious an offense this might seem to priests than to people. The train came down from Coal City and passed them while they dressed, making a great deal of happy and vigorous noise, but it only sharpened their realization that by now everybody was up and around and that certain people would be looking for them and watching for them already, so that they hardly even had the heart to look up at the blank baggage car and the empty coach and to wave at the engineer who saluted them.

Richard didn't even look up as the train passed, nor had the thought of punishment very clearly entered his mind; all the while he dressed, he watched the snake. From the break on back it lay belly up and the pallor of the belly, and the different structure of the scales, so well designed for crawling, were quietly sickening to see. He tried to see all that he could see without looking at the annihilated head, but his eyes kept flicking back to where it lay, mashed almost like soft metal against the rock, almost as flat and ragged as the toadfrogs and pennies they used to put on the tracks in Knoxville, after the streetcar ran over them. The snake moved very weakly now, but strongly enough that Richard could not doubt it would keep moving, and blindly experiencing the agony of death, straight on through the morning and the Three Hour Service and on through the afternoon until, at last, as the top rim of the sun sank out of sight, the tip of the tail would give one last quaver and the snake would lie still forever.

"Well come on," he was startled to hear Hobe's voice at his shoulder. He turned to go.

"Ain't you takin him?"

It had not occurred to Richard; now that it did, he certainly did not want him.

"No."

"Hell fahr, you kilt him didn you?"

"I don't want him."

Hobe and Jimmy glanced at each other. "Okay," Hobe said. He took the snake carefully by the tail. The break in the body held firm; the head pulled loose from the rock like adhesive

tape. He snapped him like a whip; now most of
the head was lost.

"He'll bust in the middle," Jimmy said.

"Hell I keer," Hobe said. But he did not snap
the snake again. Half a snake wouldn't be worth
showing.

On the far side of the track they fell into single
file for the woods path, Hobe ahead, swinging the
limpid snake at the new leaves, then Jimmy, then
Richard. Without consulting or imitation, all
three had put their shoes on when they dressed;
they walked rather quickly, and they did not talk.

In refusing the snake, Richard realized, he had
lost a considerable portion of their esteem, though
not all of it. He was still regarded as the hero of
this occasion and he knew he was still one of them
in a way he had never been before. He was still
pleased to have been accepted and still pleased
with his own courage, though he was sorry the
snake had been killed, and unhappy and uneasy
whenever he caught a glimpse of it ahead. He
began to know how very hungry he was and with
his hunger he remembered once again, with sur-

prise and shame that he could have forgotten,
what Day this was. It must be on past seven
o'clock by now. He would not start carrying the
Cross until nine. By now He would just be sitting on the stool or the bench in the garrison
room, probably sort of like a locker room, while
the soldiers paid Him no attention much but just
hogged their breakfasts and maybe threw cornbread at Him, no it wouldn't be cornbread; He
just sat there with nothing to eat or drink and
some of the worst things were already over by
now; He sat in the purple robe holding the reed
and the blood was drying on His back from the
scourges and the torn wounds were itching and
the spit was drying on His face (like my hand is
drying), not just spit but the nastiest kind of
snot, too, if it happened here they'd spit tobacco
juice, and down through the drying spit the
blood ran from the Crown of Thorns; how did
they push those thorns down around His forehead without hurting their hands? And here I am,
he thought, suddenly remembering the absolute-
ness of emotions during the moments just after

he woke up that morning. Here I am. He struck his breastbone and tried to imagine how it would feel to be scourged with a cat-o'-nine-tails with lead tips, and to wear a crown of thorns. Busy with twisted and uneven walking, he could not make it very clear to himself. He closed his eyes and almost immediately stumbled on a root. Jesus falls for the first time, he said to himself. God help me. God forgive me I didn't mean it. He kept his eyes open and took care how he walked.

The woods were full of ordinary sunlight now; the colors were no longer strange and the deep perspectives were no longer mysterious, but pleasant and casual. When they came to the clearing it was full of simple light and the bird was no longer singing. When they had come nearly to the other side of this warm open silence Richard hurried back to the tree on which he had left the locust shell, detached it gently, and with great care, scarcely looking at it, settled it into the breast-pocket of his shirt. They were not far into the woods when he caught up. His trotting and quick breathing, now that he slowed again to a walk, made him aware once more of his sharp hunger. It was going to be a long day without food, without, if he could help it, even rinsing his mouth out with water. I'll help it, he told himself, imagining water in his mouth. I'll not do that, anyhow. He thought again of the thorns, and the spittle, and the patience and courage, and of his maculate hand. The least I can do, he told himself. The *least* I can do! The day lifted ahead of him very long and hard, a huge unshaded hill. The climbing of it would go on in the heavy sun without rest throughout this livelong day and forever so long as he might be alive and there at the top there was dying: His; His; so hard and so long. It won't be over till sundown, he said to himself. Such a terrible and cold heaviness distended in the pit of his stomach, and his knees became suddenly so weak, that for a few moments he had to lean against a tree, and found it difficult to breathe. He had never before known such heaviness or such cold, crushing sorrow. "*Forgive!*" he whispered, barely able to bring the word out: "*Forgive ! O God forgive!*" But the cold and enormous heaviness only increased, and the sadness now seemed more than his soul could endure.

After a little, however, he regained sufficient strength in his knees, and walked again, by now a good way behind the others. But the heaviness stayed, so that he felt as if he were carrying an all but impossible weight in the middle of his body.

By now they could see the first of the buildings through the lightleaved woods; and now the whole of the School stood up before them and the two boys ahead walked more slowly, wondering what lie, if any, might lighten their trouble. But they could not think of any that would do and when Richard overtook them, lingering unhappily at the stile, they were so far beyond hope that they didn't even bother to ask him whether he had any ideas.

Now that he was with them again, the heaviness was somewhat less severe, and he began to wonder what had made him so deeply weak and unhappy, and what kind of trouble they would be in for; now he could clearly foresee Father

Whitman's hard sleepless eyes in his first look at them as they would come up from the woods, their hair spiky with incriminating wetness; and much as he dreaded in advance the punishment, which would be a whipping for sure, he told himself, he dreaded even more the first meeting with these eyes, and the first words that would be spoken, though he suspected that these would be tempered to the day. He heard Jimmy say to Hobe that he better get rid of that snake, and he thought that he sure better; and he was neither surprised nor particularly troubled when, a few moments later, Hobe slung the snake in among the hogs. He stood with the other children at the fence and watched with interest while two of the hogs, with snarling squeals, scuffled over the snake, tore it apart at its middle wound and, while the two portions still tingled in the muck, gobbled them down. It occurred to him, with a lancing quailing of horror and pity, that the snake was still alive, and would stay alive in their bellies, however chewed, and mangled, and diffused by acids, until the end of the day; but now, remembering the head, he told himself that the snake was so far gone by now that he must be a way beyond really feeling anything, ever any more (the phrase jumped at him): (Who had said that? His mother. "Daddy was terribly hurt so God has taken him up to Heaven to be with Him and he won't come back to us ever any more.") "Ever any more," he heard his quiet voice repeat within him; and within the next moment he ceased to think of the snake with much pain. When the boys turned from the sty he followed them towards the Main Building carrying, step by step with less difficulty, the diminishing weight in his soul and body, his right hand hanging with a feeling of subtle enlargement at his thigh, his left hand sustaining, in exquisite protectiveness, the bodiless shell which rested against his heart.

RECENT FICTION TITLES BY IMPORTANT CONTEMPORARY AUTHORS FROM BALLANTINE BOOKS

NIKOS KAZANTZAKIS: "One of the great figures on the stage of world literature." (*New York Times Book Review*.) Now in print:

ZORBA THE GREEK	75¢
FREEDOM OR DEATH	95¢
THE GREEK PASSION	95¢

ANTHONY BURGESS: "The ablest satirist to appear since Evelyn Waugh." (Stanley Edgar Hyman in *The New Leader*.) Now in print:

THE WANTING SEED	60¢
HONEY FOR THE BEARS	60¢
A CLOCKWORK ORANGE	60¢
NOTHING LIKE THE SUN	60¢

DORIS LESSING: Author of *The Golden Notebook*. "One of the most powerfully equipped young novelists now writing." (C. P. Snow.) Now in print:

THE GRASS IS SINGING	60¢
THE HABIT OF LOVING	60¢
A MAN AND TWO WOMEN	75¢

ZOÉ OLDENBOURG: "The foremost living fictional interpreter of the Middle Ages." (Orville Prescott in *The New York Times*.) Now in print:

THE CORNERSTONE	95¢
DESTINY OF FIRE	95¢

To order by mail, send price of book plus 5¢ for postage and handling to Dept. CS, Ballantine Books, 101 Fifth Avenue, New York, New York 10003

THE BEST
AMERICAN SHORT STORIES
1965

edited by
Martha Foley

". . . this 1965 collection of 22 stories deserves,
I think, special praise.

It is a most honorable collection. Its stories, differing widely in subject matter, technique, tone
and effect, maintain a remarkable consistency of
excellence. There is nothing second-rate here.
Every piece shows its own fine integrity. And
all do what good stories must do: they share
through words some stretch of human experience, so that it becomes, vicariously, the reader's
own."

Richard Sullivan
—Chicago Tribune *Books Today*